TUAH

JEYDA BOLUKBASI

Jeyda K. Bolukbasi/Tuah
Printed in the United States of America

Publisher's Note: This is a work of fiction. Names, characters, places, and incidents are a product of the author's imagination. Locales and public names are sometimes used for atmospheric purposes. Any resemblance to actual people, living or dead, or to businesses, companies, events, institutions, or locales is completely coincidental.

Tuah/ Jeyda K. Bolukbasi-- 1st ed.

ISBN 9781076441225 Print Edition

Dedicated to my maternal grandparents, the inspiration for this book

- CHAPTER 1 -

THUMP, THUMP. THUMP, thump. Thump, thump.
That was the first sound I ever heard. My heartbeat.

It being the only sound in my dark world gave me a sense of peace. I never wanted to leave where I was. It was cozy and safe, and I was happy.

I began to fall back into my slumber when my ears sensed another sound. I knew from the first moment I heard it that it was my favorite sound. It was a little muffled from the shelter that enclosed me, but I could still hear every ounce of love in it. The only working senses I had were my ears and touch, so my hearing was amplified. I had no idea what words were being spoken, but that didn't matter.

All that mattered was how perfectly the sound swam out of the speaker's mouth and into my tiny ears. I imagined it flowing out like a calm, clear, river through my warm, protective shelter and into the examining world of my senses. I loved that sound. I didn't know what it was or who sang the words, but I loved it. Then, I felt a disturbance next to me. It wasn't a tender, heartfelt movement that I felt when The Singer moved, but something like competitor. It didn't care if it disturbed me, it didn't care if it harmed me. It only cared about itself and getting the love and care that it wanted and needed. I knew I was sur-rounded by kin.

Then I heard another strange, muffled sound. It was like the sound of breaking a stick underwater -- a muted crack. I lazily listened to cracks for a long time until finally it stopped, and I heard soft chirping and the singer speaking to it. I knew what it was. It was a sibling.

As time passed, more and more siblings escaped their safe shelters, but I never wanted to leave mine. I was happy here and I didn't need anything else. Until one day, my muscles started to itch for movement and my lungs yearned for the fresh, cool air outside of my safe cradle of love and safety.

My body was squished together in the most space-efficient way. My spine curved with the roundness of my home and my legs were pressed close to my stomach. My neck was bent and curled around so that my head could rest on top of my thighs and my beak could reach my stomach if I stretched it. Stubby little wings were pulled in close to my body, almost unnotice-able. My body wasn't slimy like it was in the early stages of my creation, but my feathers were smooth and fur-like from the moisture that still resided in my home. It was relatively comfy. However, I had no spare room for my legs and wings to explore.

I'm sure it wouldn't hurt to stretch a little bit, I thought. So, I chose to attempt to break my safe habitat open just a little bit to give my legs some more room. I pecked at my shell with my tiny egg tooth. Nothing. I pecked again. A clear sounding crack star-tled me, and I heard sounds that were no longer muffled flood in. One sound most of all -- the sleepy breathing of my kin and the singing of The Singer.

There was no light that entered, only sound and cool air. I gratefully inhaled my first breaths of the outside world. Suddenly, it wasn't enough. I had forgotten about the safety and warmth of my home that I loved. All I wanted was fresh air, sounds, and sights. Curiosity and instinct fueled my exhausting fight for freedom.

I pecked more and pushed blindly, trusting my instincts and stretching out little by little, until finally I was outside of my home. Not much was different. It was still dark and warm. Only, I felt like I had just come to the surface of the ocean at night after living underwater for a year.

Then, realization hit me. My first home was an eggshell, and I was a chick that had just hatched. Unexpectedly, I became very fatigued from my fight to exit the eggshell. I snuggled in next to some fluffy things in the dark place I lived and peacefully fell asleep.

I awoke to the sound of The Singer humming a melody to us. My feathers had fluffed out and dried, and I was now a cute little chick. My siblings cheeped to her as she spoke back to them.

The entire world began to move. Soft down brushed past me and the muted rustling of feathers filled my ears. Then, light! Hard, powerful light crashed onto my closed eyelids. I cringed fearfully. Slowly, I opened them. I saw two giant legs, a feathered body above me, and many more chicks like me tumbling about. Below me was grass, carefully shaped into a bowl. "Hi, Mother!" my siblings chirped merrily as they ran out from underneath her.

I managed to crawl to the front of her body and I peeked out from between The Singer's feathers. I gasped at what I saw. I couldn't believe it! It was beautiful!

I saw a hurricane of colors and wilderness. Before me were rocky, rolling hills covered in green, lively grasses and shrubs spotted with flowers. Stones were scattered around, and huge boulders protruded from the ground. The sky was a glorious blue with feathery clouds streaked across it.

The bright sun was blinding, but I continued to study the landscape. A marsh was hidden by tall grasses and as I looked closer, I saw other creatures like me. Grey bodies with long, black and white necks waddled around here and there with little gray fluffy things that cheeped following behind them. I opened my beak in wonder and joy.

"What do you think?" The Singer asked me.

I turned my head around to see her face. She was even more beautiful than her song. She had a short pink beak with a black dot on the end that looked like a dot of paint. And beautiful, loving, shiny black eyes happily gazing down at me. She had a white head and part of her long, curved neck was white, but the rest of it and the rest of her body was covered in black and white barred feathers.

I weakly tweeted back to her as I turned to look back at the land I would come to know as the Tundra. She let out a heartfelt chuckle.

"You have to speak, my gosling." She whispered as she smiled.

"It's beautiful." I said softly.

I realized I was in a nest on a small hill close to the marsh. The sun was shining on my fluffy grey feathers, but the air was still cold. Snow dotted the landscape and added a touch of white. I loved how straight the horizon was, as if it was a perfectionist and that if it was the slightest bit imperfect, it wouldn't exist at all. A cool breeze blew by and ruffled my soft, grey, downy fluff before it carried on to rustle the grass and smooth the water.

As I watched the breeze fly by, I saw my five siblings near the water with another bird that looked like The Singer.

"What is that?" I asked her inquisitively.

"That's Father," she gently said to me. "And I am Mother. Come with me."

She stood up and I wobbly fell down. She honked to Father as she shook her snowy white tail feathers. I loved how Mother and Father stood proud and tall. Father honked back and Mother began to walk towards him, leaving me alone on the nest.

- Chapter 2 -

"WAIT!" I TWEETED.

She didn't stop. I stood there on the nest and panicked. I didn't want to be alone and Mother and Father were near the water. I tweeted loudly and cried for mother to come back. When she didn't turn around, I darted towards her. I fell down many times as I waddled through the grass and later made it to the reeds. My black legs were weak and shaky.

The strange feelings of the grass startled me. It was sharp, but soft at the same time. The ground was cold and the grass was bathed in dew. I would have stopped to admire the flowers, but I was running as fast as my young legs would allow me to.

Soon, I arrived at where Mother, Father, and my siblings were. Father was floating on the water, honking at my siblings to follow. The chicks hid under Mother and I ran under her as well. I breathed a sigh of relief, thankful they had not abandoned me. She started to walk forward and my siblings and I dodged her bright, orange webbed feet. Mother happily waddled over to Father and gracefully slid into the water.

"Come!" Mother happily honked.

I was about to be trampled by my siblings when, one by one, they all sluggishly and cautiously walked into the water and swam over to Mother and Father. They tweeted and chirped loudly. I was soon the only one left.

"Come, Tuah! Come!" Mother honked as Father drifted away.

I knew I wouldn't like the water, so I quickly ran in and swam over to Mother as fast as I could. The water was cold, but I enjoyed it. It was fun!

The water rippled and moved like it was breathing. It shimmered in the sunlight like a glittery dancer. I noticed that mud lined the banks and small gosling footprints followed the paths through the grass.

My tiny, black, webbed feet paddled me through the water as I followed after my parents. The late spring air was medicinal, and I soon recovered from my traumatic and fear fueled chase after my mother. I was enjoying myself, but chatter of our flock soon became louder than my own thinking.

"Mother, I want food!" one of my siblings complained.

"Patience, chick. We're going to food." Father said in a deep, strong voice.

"Amava isn't giving me any space, Father! Tell her to move!" one of my brothers said.

"He's bothering me!" Amava cheeped.

"Get along with your sister, Eiloo." Father honked.

As we were swimming through the marsh, I saw many other nests with eggs or chicks or mothers sitting. I looked at Father and immediately wanted to be just like him. He was watchfully guiding us through the marshes with his head held high, looking out for danger. Mother was watching too, but she was mostly making sure we were all together. I loved both of them. I adored my sweet mother and I tried to copy my brave and handsome father. I stretched my neck as long as it would go and swung my head side to side as if I was looking for danger.

"What are you doing?" Eiloo asked.

"I'm Father," I tweeted.

"Why are you Father?" Eiloo laughed.

"I want to be just like him," I answered.

One of the oldest chicks looked back at us. "Ha! Little Tuah is pretending he is as important as Father!"

All my siblings started laughing. I looked down at the water and watched a teardrop plop into the marsh.

"Quiet, Heru," Mother said sternly to the sibling that laughed at me.

"It's okay, Tuah. Heru is just mean," said Eiloo.

I nodded as we silently sailed over the dark marsh water.

Soon, Father climbed out of the water onto a grassy bank and shook his tail feathers like Mother did. "Watch, chicks," he said as he began to pluck pieces of grass from the bank and eat them. He quickly but gently picked and ate small leaves that had blown here on the breeze and pieces of short grass.

"Come," he said to us after demonstrating. We all rushed out of the water to where Father was standing as Mother followed behind us.

I looked at the grass and my siblings who were practicing eating it. I cocked my head as I looked down. Another warm spring breeze blew by and the grass danced and weaved itself as the breeze blew by. It seemed alive. It was colorful and it moved, just like the water. I didn't want to eat it! What if it got sad?

I didn't want to hurt its feelings, but I was hungry. "Mother, I don't want to eat the grass," I whined.

"You have to, Gosling. How do you expect to grow with nothing to grow off?" she asked.

"But what if the grass gets sad?" I asked.

"It won't. Eat the grass, Tuah," she said less kindly.

I didn't want to make Mother sad, so I started to peck at the grass. I struggled to get it in my beak after I plucked it from the Earth. After some practice, I managed to eat many petite blades of grass. I had to eat the older grass because one of my sisters had pushed me away from the young grass. Another one of my siblings found a berry and ran away from the rest of the chicks. I watched as many of my brothers and sisters chased after it, trying to get the berry. Eventually, Father ate it to break up the argument that followed the chase.

After we had all filled our bellies, Father led us back to the nest. Mother plopped down on the nest while my siblings and I crawled underneath her. We all got comfortable under her as she started to sing us to sleep. Hearing her sing and being cooped up in a warm, sheltered place reminded me of being in my egg which I had already completely forgotten about.

- CHAPTER 3 -

"WAKE UP, TUAH!" Eiloo chirped. I opened my eyes and looked at him.

"Why?"

"We can go play!" he answered. We crawled out from underneath Mother while she got off the nest and sat next to where my siblings and I were playing. Father sat down and took a nap -- he had been guarding Mother while we were napping. There were many geese families around us, so we had lots of other chicks we could play with.

I followed Eiloo to a small hill where we could get a better view of our location. We climbed up it and saw many more geese on their nests with their chicks around us. "Look at all of them!" I cheeped. We were on the edge of the flock of geese.

"Who is that?" Eiloo asked as his beak pointed to a goose like Mother surrounded by chicks.

"Let's go see," I said. We waddled deeper into the group, towards the goose. I heard honks and tweets and I saw downy feathers spread out on the ground. Something pecked me hard from behind me and pulled a bundle of downy feathers out of my back.

I squeaked and turned around to see a mother goose on a nest hissing, "Stay away from my eggs, Gosling!"

I quickly ran after Eiloo and tripped over a rock when I arrived next to him. He was standing in a group of other chicks around a very old goose. "Who is that?" I asked Eiloo.

"I think he is telling us legends," he cheeped back.

I listened to the elderly goose whose head was a brownish grey instead of my mother and father's snowy white heads. He was standing on faded orange legs with his aging eyes wide open as he spoke to us. "Have any of you heard the story of the goose, Vivir?" he asked. His voice was childlike and lively, and his expressions were animated.

We all shook our heads with our beaks wide open with excitement. "Well, Vivir was a chick like you, but he never listened to his mother and father. They told him to stay close to his mother, they had sensed danger. But, Vivir didn't listen and he ran away from his parents to find food. His parents yelled for him to come back, but he wouldn't. Soon after he had left them, he saw a red fox!" the elder goose said.

"What is a fox?" one of the chicks asked.

"A sly and dangerous creature! They prey upon geese and goslings. When Vivir saw the fox, he ran back to his parents as fast as he could, but the swift animal caught Vivir!" he said. Everyone gasped. I heard an adult chuckle behind us. "He cried and cried but his mother and father didn't come running to save him. The fox carried Vivir to his den and just before he fed him to his pups, Vivir cried out, 'I am sorry I did not listen to my parents! I will listen to them for the rest of my life and never disobey them again if you free me!'

"The fox thought about what Vivir had said. His pups needed

food, but Vivir's words were genuine. So, he took Vivir's wings and fed them to his pups, but freed Vivir! He returned to his parents, but never flew to the wintering grounds, or anywhere else," the ancient goose finished.

Everyone was silent with awe. "What does this story teach us?" the goose asked.

"To listen to our parents!" everyone called out.

"Yes," he said, "and to avoid foxes."

Another old goose approached us. "Now go back home to your mothers and fathers, goslings. It's getting late," she honked.

"Let's go tell everyone about Vivir," Eiloo cheeped to me. We ran back to our nest where Mother and Father were waiting for us. The sun had begun to set, and made the whole world look beautiful. A light as orange as Mother's scaly legs covered the marshes.

"Come on!" Eiloo said as I was marveling at the sunset. He pulled me underneath Mother who was already on the nest with the other chicks. After we had all snuggled up together, Eiloo and I told everyone about the story of Vivir, missing a few key points and details, then we listened to Mother's sweet song lulling us to sleep.

The next morning, we all awoke to a beautiful sunrise but almost no water in the marsh. I was breathless from the beauty of the marsh and the geese that were bathed in rich, orange, morning sunlight.

"Where is the water, Mother?" Suma, one of my siblings cheeped.

"The tide is out. We have to walk to the grass today," Mother honked.

Mother and Father started to waddle to the mud where the water was, their tails swinging back and forth as their legs stepped onto the short marsh grass. We followed them, our little tails flipping back and forth, and our little legs running to keep up. When I stepped on the mud, my feet felt really strange. The mud was cold and slippery. It stuck to my webbed feet as I struggled to keep up. I looked back and saw the shape of my feet in the mud, along with my sibling's and my parents.

"Eiloo, look!" I called to him. He turned around and looked at what my beak was pointing at.

He ran back to me. "Cool!" he tweeted. "Hurry, we need to keep up! We don't want a fox to get us!" he said with a touch of fear. We both took off towards our parents on short, black legs.

We arrived at a patch of grass with a small bush with berries growing on it. There was another family of geese there, and we fed next to them. I picked up one of the berries and examined it. After looking at it for a second, I swallowed it like everyone else was doing. I squeaked in happiness. The berry was much better than the grass! I began to eat more berries, but then I heard a gosling speaking from the other family.

"Mommy, Zua won't let me have a berry!" she cried.

"Just eat grass," her mother answered.

The other chick seemed really upset, and I decided to bring her a berry to make her feel better. I looked at my mother and father and they weren't watching me. I picked up a berry from our side of the bush and walked over to the gosling who was eating grass sadly. Everyone loved the berries because they were sweeter than grass.

"Here," I cheeped through a beak with a berry in it.

She looked up at me. I put the berry on the ground next to her.

"Thank you!" she said happily, blinking away tears. She enthusiastically gulped the berry down. "What is your name?" she chirped.

"Tuah. What's yours?" I asked.

"Lexa."

"Tuah?" Father honked nervously.

"I have to go," I cheeped to Lexa.

"Goodbye. And thank you!" she said.

I waddled over to Father. "Tuah!" he said when he saw me. "You scared me."

"Sorry, Father," I said. His head dropped to the ground as he continued to eat.

- CHAPTER 4 -

MANY DAYS PASSED LIKE this, Eiloo and I growing closer and our feathers growing in. I never saw Lexa over this time and I learned all the elder goose's stories. Mother and Father took very good care of us. I still loved them as much as I loved my new feathers. Grey feathers were replacing the soft hatchling down and my short newly grown tail was white. My yellow legs were still very yellow-black, but they were becoming orange. My black beak was grey and the slightest bit pink. My wing feathers were still growing in and I loved waking up in the morning and seeing how much they had opened up overnight.

I wasn't a tiny chick anymore, but I was a little less than half of my father's size. Eiloo and I grew very close with one of our siblings named Parus, and she made sure we always got along.

We spent months together in the marsh. I still enjoyed the sunrise and sunset as much as the first time I had seen it. Eiloo and I would play together every day and occasionally let Parus in on what we were up to. I loved growing up on the Tundra.

The three of us went out to find some grass to eat together one cloudy day. That day, we got our first taste of real life. We all had our heads looking down at the ground, eating grass and anything else we could find. Eiloo and I were next to each other, but Parus was farther away from us. I thought I heard the sound of wingbeats above me, but I didn't think it was anything more than another goose. Suddenly, Parus screamed from behind us and Eiloo and I spun around. A jaeger was attacking Parus! It must have been hovering above us and dove, trying to knock her unconscious so that it could carry her away. Eiloo and I screamed too, and jumped into the sky to flee, only to come back down to Earth a second later.

The jaeger was much bigger than us and he started to fly off with Parus as his talons ripped her feathers. I finally got a good look at the predatory bird. It had the body of a gull, but its head was capped in black. It had a white breast and long, tapered wings for aerodynamic mastery. He had webbed feel like us, only the claws on the end of his feet were longer and sharper than ours. He had a short tail, but two long feathers sticking out from the end of his tail, creating the impression of swords on a body ready for battle.

"Run, boys!" Parus screamed as she struggled and called for help from our parents. The jaeger was struggling to lift her into the sky. She was fighting with all her might to escape the jaeger's grip. It was finally able to lift itself up from the ground and out of nowhere, Father appeared and ripped the jaeger out of the sky. He was viciously hissing at it and yelling for us to run back to our mother while he struggled to free Parus. He clawed at the jaeger and managed to move Parus behind him.

Before we could get too far away, Father had the jaeger flying away without Parus. We ran back to see what happened. There were piles of feathers floating to the ground Parus was shaking and hiding underneath Father's wing as we watched the bird glide away.

"Thank you, Father," I heard Parus say.

We told Mother and our siblings what had happened as Mother fixed Parus's feathers up. Mother was shocked, but Parus was still as feisty as she was before she had been attacked. I told everyone about how amazing Father was when he saved her, but I kept to myself how much I wanted to be just like him one day. I looked up to him more that I looked up to the stars every night when I dreamed of the future. But, throughout my teen years, I became more worried that I wouldn't become as much like my father as I aspired to be.

A few weeks later, I was preening my new feathers on the cold marsh water while everyone was spread out eating in the warm morning light. I pulled my neck close to my body and curved it as I closed my eyes to nap. Then, I heard a familiar voice on the bank. I opened my eyes and turned my head towards the bank. To my surprise, I saw Lexa sitting on the bank with her family! I smiled to myself and started to swim to her, but then I got an idea. Before she saw me, I found a berry bush and picked a berry up in my beak.

I walked through the marsh grasses behind her and as she turned around, I dropped the berry at her feet. She smiled as warm as the morning light when she recognized me. "Tuah!"

"Hello, Lexa," I said.

She looked down at the berry. "Thank you," she said as the ate the berry. "I haven't seen you in such a long time," she said after she ate the berry.

"Where were you all those weeks?" I asked.

"My nest is a few berry bushes that way," she said as she pointed North with her beak.

Her feathers had changed as well. She wasn't tiny and fluffy any more, her grey feathers had started to grow in, and she even had a few white feathers on her head. She was older than me and her tail was fully grown and beautifully white.

"Where did you get the berry?" she asked.

I pointed with my beak to the direction where I found it. "Can we go there?" she tweet-honked like all of us did at this age.

"Do you need to ask your Mother?"

"She knows my call if she needs me," she replied, smiling. "Let's go."

We swam over to the berry bush and ate berries together until we couldn't eat any more. We talked all evening and caught up on everything that had happened since the last time we met. We seemed to share to many similarities and interests. "I should go home, Tuah," Lexa said when we had finished.

"Me too."

"See you later. I live over there, remember?" she said as she pointed North again.

"Yes. And I live on that small hill," I answered.

She nodded. "Goodbye, Tuah. And thank you," Lexa said.

"You're welcome," I replied as she walked into the water, heading towards her nest. I turned around as well and headed home.

- CHAPTER 5 -

"WHAT'S HER NAME?" Parus asked excitedly when I had returned to the nest.

"Who's name?" I asked.

"I know you were with a girl! You're always back to the nest on time! And I can see it in your eyes. I know you better than you do, brother." she answered.

"Just be quieter, Parus," I said, rolling my eyes.

Eiloo walked over to us. "What's going on?" he asked.

"You remember when we went to that berry bush a long time ago? I met someone there and I happened to see her today and we hung out some. But she's just a friend. And don't tell anyone!" I didn't want to give my older siblings any more reasons to pick on me.

Parus laughed. "I'll see if I can keep my beak shut," she said as she walked to the nest and got comfortable next to everyone else.

"I won't tell anyone," Eiloo promised. He followed Parus.

I sat next to Heru to sleep. He pecked me angrily telling me to go away, and I jumped up and sat next to Parus. I sighed.

"He's the oldest chick," she said. "He is allowed to do that."

"Everyone's allowed to do that to me," I answered.

"Well, Eiloo and I don't," she replied.

I closed my eyes for the night. "At least I have two geese who I can trust will love me," I said.

Parus was quiet for a minute. "I won't tell anyone about her," she said quickly as she closed her eyes.

"Thanks."

∼

I went to Lexa's nest every day after that. We felt the weather cool as we would float together on the marsh water or walk together on the mud during low tide. Sometimes we would eat berries together and talk about the first time we met. She told me that we lived on the Tundra and I told her that Tundra was a beautiful name and that it fit our beautiful home perfectly. We wondered if the wintering grounds were as glorious as the spring breeding grounds we now lived on.

I was excited about migration. I had never migrated before, but I had heard that it a magnificent thing. All emperor geese migrated together for the winter and we would return when the weather warmed up. I loved to dream about migration with Lexa and how I wanted to see the world. She enjoyed the breeding grounds and they gave her a sense of home and safety, too. I agreed with her, but I still was excited to be able to fly. I liked being with Lexa and I hoped that we would be able to travel to the wintering grounds together. It didn't really matter if I couldn't migrate with her, because I would find her in the wintering grounds anyway.

"Come, goslings," Mother said to us one day in Autumn.

We all walked up to her from where we were feeding. Father was with her next to the nest. "Are my chicks ready for migration?" she asked.

"We still have a month, Mother," Amava said.

"Yes, I know. But we have to prepare. The elder is going to teach all young fledglings about humans before we migrate. In a couple of weeks, your father and I will teach you how to fly and we will have the ceremony. I am so proud of you. Every single one of my hatchlings survived and grew up." She laughed, "even Parus." Parus smiled.

"This evening we will go to the elder and he will teach you about humans. Preen, please. I want my babies looking nice. I'll call you when it's time to go," she finished.

While we waited, I decided to talk to Eiloo while we watched the sun set. We sat next to each other while we looked at the sun through the marsh grasses. "It's sad that we are going to leave," I said.

"We can go with Mother and Father to the wintering grounds and come back, but you know we can't stay together forever," Eiloo answered.

"I'm going to miss you, Eiloo. You've been the best brother anyone could ask for."

"I loved having a little brother like you. If you didn't exist, I would be the youngest and everyone would peck at me all the time. At least I have one sibling to peck at!" he said as he softly pecked me.

I smiled. "I love you, Eiloo," I said.

"I love you too."

"I remember hearing everyone hatch. It's amazing that I heard you hatching but it's impossible to know which one was you. Every peck at every egg seemed to come from different birds every time," I said.

"I wish I would have seen you hatch. You hatched at night, though," Eiloo answered. I nodded.

"Come, goslings!" Father called. We stood up and walked to where Father was. Once we had all grouped together, we followed him to the middle of the group of geese where the elder goose was. He was surrounded by many others, but when is he not?

Everyone was standing in a circle, waiting for him to begin. There were mostly fledglings, but there were adults too. I got a good view of the elder, but Heru pushed me to the side and took my spot. There was nothing I could do but try to see through the crowds. I looked for Lexa but I couldn't find her. Then, the elder started speaking, his old eyes wide as usual.

"Welcome everyone. First, I would like to give you a few tips on migration. Remember, it is a difficult journey. Be prepared for that. There will be different foods in the wintering grounds too. Begin to eat more than usual to get ready for migration so that no one dies of starvation. There will be new dangers during migration and in the wintering grounds, including humans. Now, what is a human?" he asked the group of young geese.

"A predator," someone said.

"Yes. They are the most dangerous predator for geese or any animal. I have learned over my years not to try to describe to young geese what humans look like. But I will say to never approach one. They are deadly. Their main weapon is the death-berry. It is a grouping of small berries that the humans shoot at us. They let out a warning boom just before they hit. If you hear it, fly as far away as possible. Be careful on bodies of water near where humans live and watch out when you are flying. We have no defense against them," the elder finished.

The speech was concise, but essential. Humans sounded deadlier than anything I had ever imagined before. I never wanted to encounter a human. We returned to the nest together, chatting about the speech. Everyone found their resting places and dreamed about migration.

The next morning, I swam over to where Lexa's nest was. Her mother was there fixing up her nest. "Excuse me?" I asked.

She looked up and cocked her head. "Yes?" she said.

"My name is Tuah. Where's Lexa?" I asked.

"Why?" she said questioningly. "We met in the Spring and I wanted to talk to her before migration," I answered.

She seemed to lower her guard. "She went that way to eat," Lexa's mother said. She pointed to the right.

"Thank you," I replied. She nodded.

I started walking in the direction she had pointed. I walked for a long time without finding Lexa. I began to feel worried and started calling for her. All I could see was grass and marsh for miles. Then, I heard her make a high-pitched honk. I ran in the direction I heard her call until I heard her start her alarm call. I began to panic, running even faster towards her. My heart was beating faster than it ever had before and my wobbly goose feet struggled to keep up with my body. I even flapped my wings some to gain a little bit of lift to make me move faster. I prayed she was okay.

When I saw her I relaxed, but my heart rate picked back up when I saw an eagle flying around her, preparing to land! The elder goose had taught us about eagles and how dangerous they were. Lexa was still calling her alarm call as the eagle landed next to her. She was hiding in the marsh grasses, unseen, but the eagle was moving closer. It would have been stupid for her to run, because the eagle would easily catch up with her. The only way to escape an eagle is to fly, and neither of us could fly yet.

As the eagle was walking closer to her, I crept through the grass. My grey plumage blended in with the mud and camouflaged me. I got closer to the eagle and studied its body. The huge creature had dark brown feathers and a black tail. The base of the tail feathers were white and some of the leg feathers were white as well. The talons were as yellow as the sun and the beak was the same color. But what struck me the most was the neck. The back of the bird's neck was streaked with golden feathers.

I continued to creep up behind it. Lexa was still hiding in the grass and the eagle was looking around and searching for her. Its head was turning around and studying the environment. Its fierce eyes were determined to find Lexa. The eagle continued to move closer to her. I didn't know why I wasn't running away like I should have. Something seemed to be controlling my actions, but I didn't know what it was. Finally, I had circled the eagle and walked up behind it. He was in a small clearing, so I would have to exit my cover before reaching him. Slowly, I crept out of the reeds and walked into the clearing. I was walking on mud, so I was very quiet. I silently walked closer and closer until finally, the eagle was right in front of me. He was hunched over with his wings tucked in, looking into the reeds. I could almost feel the warmth from his body. Without thinking, I leaped on its back with my claws outstretched and startled it. He let out a loud shrill screech as my small goose claws pulled out two clumps of dark brown feathers. After flinging me off, he swung his golden head around and threw his talons at me.

"Tuah!" Lexa screeched from the reeds as she walked out.

I dodged the eagle's razor-sharp talons and he landed with a thump on the mud. I peeked back to make sure Lexa was okay. She looked fine, though she looked like she had been dodging the eagle for a little bit.

As soon as I turned around, the eagle was flying at me with his talons outstretched and grabbed me before I could dive away. I honked as his talons sunk into my young flesh. I struggled to escape his firm grip, but he was latched onto my almost-grown wing feathers.

Instinctively, I started to flap my other wing to try to take off. Then, the wing feathers the eagle was holding onto pulled out and I crashed onto the ground. I looked at my wing. Some of the young blood feathers were bleeding and broken, and I began to worry that I would not be able to grow them back in time for migration and I would be left here over the winter.

I heard the eagle screech and looked up to see that Lexa had flown up to the eagle's side while he was distracted and pecked his eye. He shook his head flung her onto the ground. The eagle screeched again. After a few moments of pained calling, he took off into the sky, dragging his huge talons behind him.

"Are you okay?" Lexa asked me worriedly as she ran over to me.

"No," I answered. My wing was hurting terribly and blood was dripping onto the grass. She walked closer to me and inspected my wing.

"Oh no."

"It's okay," I answered. "At least you're fine."

"I'll walk with you back to your nest. Your Mother needs to look at that."

- CHAPTER 6 -

"TUAH!" MOTHER SCREAMED ONCE we reached the nest. She ran towards me and looked at my wing.

Eiloo was at the nest as well and he ran over to me too. "What happened?" he asked.

Lexa answered before I could speak. "It was an eagle. It attacked me and I called for help and Tuah came and saved me. I am okay but his wing is badly hurt."

"You saved her?" Mother asked me with her eyes opened wide.

"She made the eagle fly away, but I distracted it so she could peck its eye."

"Come to the nest. We need to take care of that wing," Mother said. "Arcus!" Mother honked to my father. His head swung towards me and he rushed over.

"Well done, Tuah!" Amava honked.

"I can't believe you did that." Said Parus.

Suddenly, I was surrounded by my siblings, some wanting to congratulate me, others just wanting to see what was going on. Father brought me some food but returned to his teachings with the older males in the family after that. I hoped my father would praise me for once. I felt like he pushed me away because I wasn't like my older brothers. Yes, I was feminine, caring and kind, but I never got from him what my brothers did.

"I can't do much, Tuah. Just rest some and don't move around too much. We can only hope that the blood clots soon." Mother said.

"Do you think I will make it to the wintering grounds on time?" I asked.

"I hope so."

"Why didn't you just run away, Tuah?" Eiloo asked. I shrugged. He looked at Lexa but kept his promise that he wouldn't tell anyone else about our relationship. I wasn't too worried about not being able to migrate in time, I was just happy that nothing had happened to Lexa.

When it was time for my siblings to learn to fly, I was unable to practice in worry that I might damage my healing feathers. So, I watched my siblings and many other young geese fledge for the first time. Parus and Eiloo didn't want to leave my side, but Mother and Father convinced them to practice flying.

I sadly watched my mother and father joyously lead the rest of my family into the sky as they had their first true taste of freedom. Little did I know, I wouldn't get the luxury of tasting the sky in the cool Autumn air, I would have to learn in the middle of a snowstorm, battling the Alaskan winter.

Lexa never gave into her parent's luring or demands. She stayed with me and made sure no predators came near me while I was healing. Countless times I had asked her to leave and she had refused. I begged her to migrate on time and leave me, but she still stayed. Soon, my siblings came to say goodbye and left to migrate with many other groups of geese. I felt very scared watching everything I had ever known fly away while the first flurries of snow silently drifted onto my feathers.

~

I woke up, shivering from the frigid, early winter air. Lexa and I were nestled next to each other, trying to conserve heat. It didn't seem to make up for the bitter, stinging wind from the North. My body feathers weren't nearly enough to keep me warm, but my wing feathers were almost healed. I stretched my neck up in the freezing morning air.

The land was dark and the grass was a dormant brown. I didn't like being the only ones on the breeding grounds. It was way too quiet and still and occasionally a scavenger would search tirelessly for a tiny morsel of a chick that may have died this year. Lexa and I always hid as quietly as we could during those times, because we knew that I could become one of those chicks that died this year.

The marsh water had clear ice on the shallow edges and the dew on the brown grass had frozen into the frost that covered everything, including Lexa and me. I felt so guilty for being unable to fly and making her want to stay with me. I wished she had gone with the others to the wintering grounds, but now we were both living off dead grass and freezing our tails off in the day and almost dying at night as the temperature plunged to around negative ten degrees Fahrenheit. I knew we would have to leave as soon as possible, or we would perish.

One morning, Lexa and I had noticed powerful wind and snow coming from the Northeast and we began to panic. It would be the first winter blizzard, and we wouldn't survive the harshness of the icy snow being blasted into our faces or the fact that we wouldn't be able to escape once the storm grasped the land.

We spent that morning scavenging for the little food that was still left. The dead grass was bitter and stiff. There were no more berries and all the leaves had been frozen into little crisps. "Hey, Tuah!" Lexa yelled to me. I immediately panicked and raced to where she was.

"What is it?" I asked when I got to her. I was still panting from my run.

"I found green grass!" I sighed and relaxed. Couldn't she have yelled to me what she found instead of letting me freak out and run here? I looked down at what she was looking at and my hopes died down.

"What are you talking about? That's a poisonous weed." I recognized the plant from my teachings with Mother.

"Oh. So we can't eat it?"

"No," I answered. Lexa groaned. We spent the rest of that day with empty bellies and disappointed spirits. Two weeks passed like this and survival became even more difficult. My guilt became worse as well.

Another morning came, with the blizzard growing closer. The sun hadn't risen, the clouds were covering the sky. I was covered in frost and I stood up to shake the snow from last night's precipitation off my back.

I peeked at my wing feathers as I did every morning knowing that if they weren't fully healed, I would die and Lexa would
likely die with me. We would freeze to death if we didn't starve
first. I slowly stretched out my frost covered wing into the frigid
atmosphere. Before I looked, I thought that if I did die, it would
have been my fate anyway. Being the youngest chick, my chances for survival were slim, and now I was truly understanding
that. I had been kicked around all my life and left behind countless times. Maybe my lucky chances were up. Lexa was not the
youngest chick, and she would have probably survived her first
year if I had never given her that berry. But if we weren't meant
to be together, she would make the choice to leave. And it didn't
really matter to the world if I died. Many geese die every year,
especially youths like me.

My beak dropped and I stared in awe at my wing. They were
unpreened and frozen, but the feathers had finished healing
overnight. The shafts had opened up and created complete adult
wing feathers. Each feather had its own place and purpose. Every individual was just as important as the next. Finally, I could
learn to fly. I had prepared myself to die, and now I wasn't! I
quickly woke Lexa and showed her my wing.

"Tuah! That's wonderful!" She said. A strong gust of wind
blew past us. The storm was picking up and I could now see
deep gray clouds on the horizon. Lexa and I turned to face the
approaching clouds.

"You have to learn to fly, though, Tuah. We have to hurry!"
she honked.

I started to frantically flap my wings and hop around, but I never got more than a foot above the ground. My feathers made a deep whizzing sound as I flapped them. Snow flurries took flight around me and created the impression of dust settling around me when I stopped. I used a lot of energy flapping around, and I realized how difficult this might be.

"No, Tuah," Lexa said. "Run and flap rhythmically and slowly lift your feet off the ground. You have to feel the wind underneath your wings lifting you up and you have to use your tail to maneuver. Watch."

She took off running into the marsh with her wings outstretched. After she reached a certain speed, she started to flap her wings strongly and pushed off the ground and took off. She turned and glided back to me. "Like that," she honked after a bumpy landing.

I looked at Lexa, then at the storm which was growing closer by the minute. "You should just leave while you can, Lexa. You don't need to risk staying here any longer when you can fly to the wintering grounds."

She touched my wing with hers. "We're in this together," she answered strongly.

"Lexa, please. Why are you doing this?"

"You saved me from the eagle," she answered. "I owe you my life."

"You don't have to repay that debt, Lexa. Do you really think I can make it through the winter?"

"Don't you know what hope is? I have been telling you this ever since the eagle attacked me. I know you can make it if you just have hope. Will you believe in yourself for me?" she asked.

I almost asked her if she would leave again, but the look in her face silenced me. I agreed to keep trying, but I didn't still didn't believe that she was staying with me because I saved her from the eagle.

Once again, I felt the agonizing feeling that my injury would cause the death of another bird.

- CHAPTER 7 -

"FLAP HARDER!" LEXA YELLED from an empty frozen distance with nothing but death between us. I could not see her, the blizzard was raging around us and our only connection was voice. I grunted angrily when the wind blew me off my course back to Lexa and slammed me into the ground on my back.

"Tuah!"

"I'm coming!" I honked. I flap-hopped to where Lexa's voice came from and eventually saw her. Icy snow was being blown into my eyes and it was slowly covering my nostrils and making breathing difficult. The cruel wind continued pulling the oxygen away from me then blasting me with more air I could not catch with my lungs.

"We have to go!" I yelled above the storm. The dead grass was already covered in snow and ice along with our wings and tails.

"Are you sure you're ready?" she asked when we met up again.

I nodded. "I better be. Which way is South?" I asked.

"I don't know. We'll take off and get out of the blizzard, then we'll find the way to go. Put your back to the direction the wind is coming from the strongest and start running when I say go," Lexa answered. We both put our backs to the wind and spread out our wings. In the darkness, I was able to see flurries of snow flying past me in spirals.

"Go!" Lexa screamed. We both took off running down the hill where I was hatched and onto the fully frozen marsh, the claws on the ends of our webbed feet scraping the ice and digging into the frozen earth.

"Start flapping and jump!" Lexa said as she flapped her wings, jumped, and pulled her legs up underneath her soft downy feathers. She gained height, fighting the blizzard and intercrossing gusts of freezing winds.

I flapped my wings as hard as I could and jumped up as I pulled my legs underneath my lukewarm belly feathers. I flapped up and down and to the side as the wind blew at me from below as well as everywhere else. I struggled to stay in a straight line as I followed Lexa into the clouds. The wind tossed me around here and there, but I managed to stay in the air. I looked down to see how high I had traveled but my heart raced as I saw only snow flurries and hail falling.

I flapped as hard as I could and exhausted my tail because the tail is like the rudder, determining the direction I fly. With the wind blowing in all different directions, it was hard to keep upright and keep flying straight. Then, the ice started to fall in the clouds. Tiny shards of ice, sharper than glass, scraped at my body and forced my eyes to shut. I was lost in the storm.

I just flapped and flapped and flapped as hard as I could and hoped I was going up. The sounds of the wind and ice filled my ears and I began to lose my balance in the sky.

"Tuah!" I heard Lexa scream.

"Lexa!" I screamed back. She was somewhere near me and I dared to open my eyes but was forced to close them again as ice shards flew by.

"Take the very strong gust and glide!" Lexa yelled as her voice faded.

"What gust?"

Suddenly, an extremely-strong wind grabbed me and pulled me into it. "Woah!" I yelled as it pushed me through the sky.

I was still blind and very scared. Too much of the wind blew over my left wing and jerked it down. I fell towards the ground on my side and opened my eyes to get myself realigned with the horizon that wasn't there, so I flapped the opposite direction that gravity was pulling. Before I thought it would, the very strong gust grabbed me again and this time, I stayed in its grasp until I exited the storm.

"Lexa!" I yelled into the sky and heard no response. Now, I was truly panicking that I was alone in the storm.

I must have flown for many miles. Slowly, the blizzard let up as I exited the storm cloud. I could now see where I was flying and where I was. I must have traveled to the West, North, or South because I could see the magnificent Pacific in the distance. I looked down and saw Alaska covered in winter's blanket. I looked behind me and saw the vicious blizzard slowly blowing my direction. The clouds were a dark navy on the bottom and fluffy white on the top.

I saw the sun as high as it would go in the winter which wasn't even halfway across the sky. Then, I remembered that I had lost Lexa. I suddenly felt very alone and worried for her. Why did she have to stay with me? I probably wasn't meant to make it to the wintering grounds anyway. I desperately hoped that she was okay and that I would meet her at the wintering grounds. I would have no luck finding her, so I decided to head South and pray that she would make it there too. I judged my location and let my navigational instinct take over. I turned Southward as I slowly descended. I was starving from trying to survive off only dead grass, but I didn't want to completely land because my wings were too weak to take off again. So, I glided South as the weak Alaskan sun set. I now completely relied on the stars and my instinct.

I was exhausted, starving, and freezing, but I flew on. The land seemed dead with only the resilient winter animals living here. The mountains were covered with snow and ice and the pine trees swayed when the cold wind blew by. Everything was either freezing or covered in snow. The air in the atmosphere was thin, but my body was well equipped for high altitude flight. The mountains towered above everything and rolled like a turbulent ocean that had been frozen in time. I grunted as the muscles on my wings burned with fatigue. I would have to land; I couldn't fly along most of Alaska's west coastline with no rest.

Soon, I reached the last leg of my journey that was over ocean. I decided to land on the marshy coastline to rest before I crossed the water. I glided down onto the salty marsh with a bumpy and painful landing. I gasped when my legs didn't catch the ground and I fell forward onto my chest. My face plummeted into the snow-covered Earth. Once I stood up again, I gathered my thoughts. I would have to find a safe place to rest, I was easy prey for any predator. A weak, hungry, and cold first-year goose really didn't have a good chance of survival, especially since I didn't have the mass of many other geese around me, alert for danger. I'll just rest for a few minutes, I thought to myself. I dipped my beak to the ground and sat down as I plucked dormant grass in the estuary while heavy snow fell from the sky.

I woke up late the next morning and shivered as I remembered where I was. The tide was out and last night's snow rested on the stiff, dormant grass. I was quickly able to take off towards the South. With luck, I would make it to the wintering grounds today. I flew low over the inlet and imagined hearing the bustle of the goose colony and hoped I would meet Lexa on the wintering grounds soon. The air was becoming warmer every mile I traveled and I was thankful to not be so cold anymore.

I finally watched the land behind me disappear as I flew over the ocean. This was the first time I had seen it. I loved how it rolled like a giant lake, similar to the ones on the breeding grounds, although, it was much more powerful. I seemed to be able to smell the strength it possessed in the salty air. I honked happily as I saw fish jump and follow me some. I enjoyed the salt air smoothing my feathers and making them cool and slightly sticky.

"Ha ha!" I boisterously laughed as I flew faster over the blue Pacific water. I stretched my neck out far as I flew and finally felt the freedom of flying without being murdered by the cold. I glanced at my wings and loved them. They were magical pieces of art that gave me indescribable feelings of not being held back by anything. *I can fly!* I thought for the first time.

I flew high up and dove down in happy spirals. I brushed the ocean while I let the wind control me as the ocean would if I was in the water. The wind currents pushed and pulled me and I glided along with them freely, not caring where I had been or where I was going, not really caring about anything but my new-found freedom. Maybe now, Father would see me for more than the just the youngest of the clutch.

I imagined that this was how my siblings felt when I watched them fly for the first time and I thought of how such a powerful feeling coming from so many souls could truly change the world. I loved flying and I knew that it would be one of the few things that no one could ever take away from me and that I would always have.

I listened to the wind and how it loved my wings and feathers and lifted me up higher than anything could ever lift anything else up. After months of waiting in the harsh Alaskan winter, I had finally seized my own freedom and my own place in the world. I had finally found freedom.

- CHAPTER 8 -

THEN, I HEARD IT. The sound of the colony on the cold rocky shores of the wintering grounds. I flew faster as the rocks grew closer along with the sounds and smells of my own kind. "I made it!" I said to myself.

Soon, I saw many geese in a few large groups spread out over the rocky land. Black and white geese blended in with the light, falling snow. Small, rocky islands surrounded the mainland and perched on them were flocks of geese, their heads tucked close to their bodies, trying to stay warm. The ocean crashed up against the larger rocks and sent freezing mist everywhere. Heads shook and flung more saltwater everywhere when the waves crashed. The snow gave the landscape a mystic look. "Lexa!" I yelled as I flew over the colony. I scanned the geese as quickly as I could, looking for her. None of them seemed to look like Lexa, and I started to panic again, thinking she didn't make it or that she stayed in the wintering grounds looking for me. Please let her be here, I thought to myself. "Lexa!" I screamed as loud as I could.

"Tuah!" I heard a voice honk behind me through the crowds. I spun around in the air and saw my mother on the ground looking up at me proudly and crying from happiness.

"Mother!" I said as I dropped down on the black, salt-covered rocks.

"You're flying!" she said as she embraced me. "Oh, my baby! You made it! I was so worried I'd never see you again! You learned how to fly!" she said through tears.

"Yes, my wing finished healing just in time."

"Oh, thank goodness you made it back okay." She said.

"Where is Father and everyone else?"

"They're this way, I'll bring you to them." She took off into the sky and I jumped up with her into the air. Flying felt so easy now that I didn't have a great distance to travel by myself. I felt like I could just float.

We flew over a few miles of coastline and geese. The wintering grounds didn't have the slightest resemblance of the spring breeding grounds, except for the geese. The snow had stopped falling and the waves were washing it away as the tide slowly moved in. Soon, we landed on the mainland and I was reunited with the rest of my family.

"Tuah, you made it!" Eiloo said when he saw me. He jumped up into the air before I could land and we dropped down together while he wrapped his wings around me and hugged me. "I'm so glad you're okay, little brother."

Father welcomed me back but didn't embrace me like mother and Eiloo. I was disappointed that he wasn't as proud of me as I had expected. I had hoped that now that I had proved how strong I was, from surviving an eagle attack and coming to the wintering grounds late, I could get praise from my idol. The rest of my siblings hugged me and welcomed me back except for the older ones. I never learned why they thought they were so much better than me. Suddenly, I thought something seemed to be missing. Parus! The happiness quickly faded from me as I assumed the worst.

"Eiloo, where is Parus?" I asked. His smile faded as well as everyone else's and I knew why Parus wasn't here. I looked down and started to weep a little with Mother. Parus had always been one of my few siblings that never picked on me like everyone else. For the rest of my life I would wonder why she had to go.

"What took her?" I asked when I looked up.

"The deathberries – humans," Eiloo answered.

"We were flying together over the land when we heard the booms that the elder goose taught us about. We scattered and tried to dodge them, but one hit Parus and she fell," Amava said quietly. Mother started to cry harder and we all hugged her.

"I guess geese only have two lives," Heru remarked.

"Not Tuah," Eiloo answered. "He survived an eagle attack, being the youngest in the clutch, and coming to the wintering grounds late. Tuah must have fifty lives."

"I need to find the goose I saved from the eagle attack. Her name is Lexa. Have you seen her?" I asked my family after a moment of silence. Everyone shook their heads.

"We will spread the word. When did you last see her?" Father asked.

"During a blizzard in the breeding grounds," I answered, surprised that he had spoken to me and was willing to help.

"Go, Tuah. You will find her," Mother said, pushing me away

with a confident look in her eyes. Mother was right. If Lexa was here, I was going to find her.

I took off away from my family. I glided over the many other geese on the rocky shoreline. Many were swimming in the water or eating algae or mussels on the rocks. My eyes were still wet from the sadness of missing the feisty little Parus and I worried that the deathberries had taken Lexa as well. I knew I couldn't go back to the breeding grounds, but she could be anywhere in Alaska by now. I hoped and hoped that I would see her somewhere in the colony. My eyes searched as hard as they could. I only saw unfamiliar geese grouped along the coastline.

I flew over the colony dozens of times, scanning as hard as I could. Once, I caught myself wondering why I was doing this. I soon remembered what she had done for me and continued to search tirelessly. The pain and soreness in my wings started to fade away and were replaced by stiffness. I was still very weak from the journey here and I needed to rest badly. I didn't have much time left to keep flying. Anxiety shot through me and I frantically looked into the distance as far as I could. I would have to land soon and would not be able to continue searching for her.

Then, I saw a weak-flying bird entering the colony from far away and I squinted my eyes to see the them better. Their flight pattern was that of a bird who seemed like they were about to stall at any moment. The bird fell onto the rocks from exhaustion and I flew over to the other side of the colony as fast as I could. When I neared, I saw it was Lexa.

"Lexa!" I yelled as I landed on the shore next to her. I nudged her with one of my feet to see if she would wake up. "Lexa?"

Her body was smaller than it used to be and I concluded that she must have been starving. Her feathers were unpreened and she was very dirty. She was laying on her back with her wings slightly outstretched.

Her head rolled over slightly and she looked at me. "Tuah!" she breathed weakly. I breathed a huge sigh of relief when she spoke.

"Rest," I whispered. "I will bring you some food when you are ready."

She nodded and fell back to sleep from her exhaustion. I tucked her wings closer to her body and moved a few rocks out from underneath her so that she was more comfortable.

～

"Tuah," she whispered.

I jumped up from where I was sitting. "Lexa?" I honked.

"We made it," she said smiling.

"Yes, we did."

"What's this?" she asked when she looked at the pile of food I had brought her.

"I couldn't find any berries for you, I'm sorry."

"Thank you, Tuah! You didn't have to do that." I nodded. Her voice was scratchy and weak.

"What happened to you?" I asked.

"Another blizzard came after I left the first one. The wind was very strong and I couldn't fly out of it. I had to hunker down and wait for it to pass. It passed quickly, but I was so worried about you. I came as fast as I could, hoping with all of my heart that you were here and I didn't sleep or eat anything the entire trip after the second blizzard left. How is your family? Have you seen mine?" she asked worriedly.

"I haven't seen yours, but I lost one of my sisters."

"Oh, I'm so sorry, Tuah."

I nodded. "Let's go find your family. Can you stand up?" I asked. Lexa stood up but fell down weakly right after. The stones slipped from underneath her when she laid down again.

"Are you okay?" I asked.

"Yeah, my legs are just tired."

"You stay here and eat. I'll find your family and bring them to you. What are your parent's names?" I asked.

"Inla and Fleiou," she answered.

I took off away from her over the colony calling their names. I traveled over many little rocky islands for hours and I worried that I wouldn't find them. I was so relieved to have Lexa back alive. I just hoped that Lexa's parents were still alive, too. Soon, I heard a honk from below me and dove down next to a mother goose. She was a small goose for our species and was very well preened. "Did you call my name, gosling?" she asked politely.

"Yes, ma'am. Are you Inla?"

"Yes," she answered.

"You're Lexa's mother?"

She thought for a minute. "Tuah?" she asked.

"Yes," I answered.

"We all thought you and Lexa wouldn't make it! Does your

mother know you are back? Please tell me Lexa -- " tears prevented her from finishing her sentence.

"Come with me, I will bring you to Lexa," I said.

She jumped into the sky as fast as she could. "Fleiou! Come! Lexa is here!" she honked loudly to her mate.

I saw another goose fly up over the rest of the geese to follow us. I quickly led them to Lexa and they rejoiced when they saw her. Lexa told them everything and I never had to breathe a word.

"Goodbye, Lexa. I will meet you tomorrow," I said when everyone had quieted down.

She curtly nodded. "Thank you, Tuah."

- CHAPTER 9 -

I LOVED LIFE IN the wintering grounds almost as much as I loved the breeding grounds. Eiloo taught me how to eat clams and mussels, and I enjoyed being on the water. Instead of floating on still marsh water, I could swim in the ocean and bob up and down and occasionally get splashed by a salt-filled wave. The rocks were enjoyable to sit on because I got a great view of the groups of other geese. In the marsh, the highest point was only a small hill.

Lexa and I spent lots of time together, we had grown closer because of what happened in the breeding grounds and during migration. We had been there for each other in hard times, and now we were still with each other during easy times. I probably flew more than any of the other first year geese. I don't think anyone ever appreciated their wings as much as I did.

But my problems didn't end when I made it to the wintering grounds. Sometimes I would wake up in the middle of the night from a nightmare. I would stare at my left wing and try to tell myself that I still had my wings. In my dreams, lots of different things would happen, but in all of them I couldn't fly. I could never fall back to sleep on those nights, so I would sit on a rock right in front of the ocean and watch the stars move while the ocean sprayed me. I loved my wings so much that I feared I would lose one of my wings and never be able to fly again, because I knew what it felt like to watch everyone I ever knew fly away and remain grounded, alone. But thoughts of Lexa helped these feelings fade away. I wasn't alone.

Then the other feeling would return. It was the thought that I would never be like my father and the memories of him never seeming to appreciate me or become connected to me. I would fail in protecting my loved ones and die alone. Why couldn't I shake these feelings?

"When will we return to the breeding grounds?" I asked Eiloo as we scavenged for clams together.

"When we're sure that winter is over. The weather will warm up and our navigational instincts will tell us it is time to go," he honked back.

"How do you know?"

"The older geese say that you will know when it comes and that you will learn to recognize it. Like, some magnetic force pulling you I guess," he answered.

"I didn't really feel it coming here. I guess the weather really tells us back at the breeding grounds," I honked.

Eiloo honked back in agreement. "Tuah, Heru has been talking about leaving Mother and Father when he gets back to the breeding grounds. Some of our older siblings have been saying that too. When do you think we should leave them?"

"Whenever it feels right, I guess."

I was the only one to watch the sun rise the next morning. I didn't really hang out with the other geese like my other brothers and sisters. They were always racing or exploring.

I spent most of my time alone or with Eiloo, but when he was gone, I was always with Lexa. I hated that I couldn't bring her berries, but I would have to wait until spring to do that. We spent most of our time together grazing on the rocks for algae. We would talk about what was going on in the flock, about the goose who saw a human near us, about returning to the breeding grounds, and wonder why there were larger rocks here than in the breeding grounds.

Most of the time it was boring in the wintering grounds. Everyone says that we are just waiting for spring and that this teaches us young geese patience. I had plenty of patience, but I felt useless just sitting around when I was not eating. It was probably because I didn't hang out with the other geese. But one day, a frail, old male goose waddled up to me on my lonely rock with the best view of the ocean.

"You okay, son?" he asked me as he walked up beside me.

"I'm fine, sir," I answered, lifting my head up from my resting.

"You're a strong goose to survive coming late. There ain't many other birds who could do that. And fly alone."

"Thank you, but I wasn't alone the whole time." I replied.

"I was a bit like you when I was younger. I was one of the youngest, but stronger than the oldest. Because I was stronger than them, my older siblings disliked me. They wanted to be the best," he honked quietly. "Are you bored here?" he asked.

"Kind of." I suddenly became very angry. "Since I came late, I missed everything! I feel cut off from my family because I wasn't with them during the first flight ritual and I didn't get to fly in a v shape with my friends and family during my first year of migration. I feel like I don't even belong here!" I yelled as I stood up. "I wake up from nightmares of not being able to fly. While my other siblings are asleep, I'm sitting here alone trying to get a hold of my feelings. I still have scars from flying through the blizzard. The only bird who truly understands what I have gone through is Lexa! I felt so... alone. Sometimes I worry that I don't appreciate her enough." I said as I sat down and dropped my head.

"We all have troubles we have to deal with. Have you ever considered leaving?" he asked.

I looked up, shocked. "Leaving?"

"Yes. You can join the Canadians. They live a good ways East from here and they dwell in larger flocks," he said.

"Then I would feel truly left out. An Emperor with Canadians?" I laughed. Although I didn't show it, I still considered his idea.

"It's your choice, gosling. Maybe if you spent time with them then returned, you would fit in better here because you will know what it is to really stand out."

"Don't they speak different?" I asked.

"Partly."

"What is your name?"

"Mounu. I've heard *your* name spoken many times in the flock," he replied.

"Good things?"

"They talk about how strong you were. No one has ever fought an eagle and escaped alive. Especially when they were defending someone else and both got out alive," he honked.

If I left, I would have to take Lexa with me. We have grown too close for one of us to leave for a long time. "Thank you, Mounu."

Mounu nodded as he stood up and waddled away.

Canadians, I thought. *Those strange black headed geese? They are fat and weird and live down south. How would I ever live with them?* I asked myself.

I woke up from another nightmare a few weeks later, but this one was different. Instead of me not being able to fly, I simply wasn't able to gain any height. Thousands of other birds were flying up in a swirling circle around me and I couldn't get off the ground. They surrounded me from the sky and the wind they blew down kept me out of the sky. I cried for them to stop but none of them heard me. I woke up from the nightmare panting with Lexa standing next to me.

"Tuah," she whispered worriedly. The moon was full and I could see all of the other geese in the wintering grounds in a calm sleep, bathed in soft, white light.

I stood up. "Come with me, Lexa." We quietly took off over the many sleeping geese and flew onto a rocky shore outside of the colony where we didn't have to whisper.

When we landed she asked, "Are you okay?"

"No, I keep having nightmares about not being able to fly."

"It's just because of what happened. You'll get over it. I know exactly how you feel. You know where I was when we were stuck in the breeding grounds- I was with you."

"No," I said sternly. "*I* was stuck in the breeding grounds. You should have left me, and you almost got yourself killed."

"I was perfectly fine! I made it here!" she honked back. "Tuah, what's up with you? You need to realize that even if you can't fly, you will be okay."

"But what if I'm not? You know how low our survival rate is."

"Who cares? We survived a blizzard, didn't we?" she asked. I realized that Lexa was right. I needed to let go of my worries.

"Thanks Lexa."

"We're in this together, Tuah," she repeated.

I had decided that I would not leave for Canada, although I would always hold the thought safe in the back of my mind. That old goose only wanted to help, and I'm sure he had considered it at some point in his life as well.

- Chapter 10-

THE SEASON HAD LAUNCHED its annual change. I felt the first warm breezes flying over the ocean brush the feathers on my face. The sun shone brighter and pulled the water on the rocks into the sky, then let it go as early spring showers fell. I showered in the fresh water and rinsed all the salt off my feathers and took a bath in the ocean afterwards. The ocean's attitude changed with the season. It rolled and tumbled with vengeance, trying to slam into the rocks as hard as it could. All the birds became more active and the adults grew their handsome breeding season feathers. I wouldn't have such marvelous feathers for two more years.

A small flock of Snow geese joined us a week before we migrated. They were beautiful birds like us, they were snowy white with black wingtips and pink bills and legs. When I was foraging for clams, I met a juvenile like me. He wasn't a beautiful white, he had a brown back but a white belly, and a white head covered in brownish-orange feathers. His beak was bigger than mine and in between the pink, there was a thick black line where it parted.

"Hi," I said as I walked up to him. He looked up at me and cocked his head. "Hey," he answered.

"My name is Tuah. Who are you?"

"My name's Bruna," he answered.

"Where did you and your flock come from?"

"America, the west coast. We flew up here to join you in migrating, but we nest farther into the Arctic Circle," he honked.

"You've been to America?" I asked eagerly.

"Oh, yeah. My dad has seen the Gulf of Mexico," he answered.

"Wow!" I said. "I was attacked by an eagle and I migrated late. My friend and I flew through a blizzard to get here," I said.

"Woah! Who is your friend?" he asked.

I suddenly became protective of Lexa. "A goose named Lexa," I answered. I decided not to tell him where she preferred to hang out. Another goose walked up behind Bruna.

"Are you talking to an Emperor, Bruna?" she asked.

"What do you think, Dailin?" he asked, almost angrily.

"Hello," I said shyly.

Dailin was a stunning Snow goose. She was a blue morph who was a year older than me. She had a navy body with white streaks on the tips of her wing feathers and she had an orange and black beak. Her eyes were perfect black spots on her white head. She seemed annoyed with Bruna and she held her head up high. "Who are you?" she asked.

"I-I'm Tuah," I stuttered.

"Dailin is one of my older sisters. She was part of a brood that hatched a year before me," said Bruna.

She was bigger than Bruna and me and it was obvious that she was almost an adult. "Come, Bruna," she said as she started to walk away.

"Dailin," Bruna started.

"W-we were just talking, Dailin," I said.

Her head swung around. "I didn't come for you, Emperor. So, unless you want to have a delayed trip to the breeding grounds too, I suggest you shut your beak. Now come, Bruna. Mother wants to talk to you," she honked.

"Sorry," Bruna whispered to me as he walked away. I nodded.

I was surprised at her harshness. "What's up with her?" I said angrily to myself once they were out of earshot. I scoffed. The last time I met something that angry and intent on killing me was when I was fighting that eagle. I flew over to where Lexa was to get away from the other geese.

"Are you ready?" Lexa asked.

"Surprisingly, I'm not scared at migrate again at all. I feel like if I could make it through what I already went through, I could fly through anything," I answered.

"Have the nightmares stopped?"

"Mostly."

"Good. Come on, I think it's almost time to go." She said.

Something seemed to ripple through the many flocks of geese and all our heads turned up to the sky. Suddenly, the hundreds of geese took off around us and we took flight. I looked down at the rocks below me and watched them fade into the morning fog and vanish. I watched my wings blow the fog away and make it curl, then it would return to that spot and I would flap at it again. I was finally flying in a flock.

Groups broke off from the flock and into v shapes. I thought we were very intelligent to fly this way, taking turns leading the flock and saving energy. Lexa stayed next to me the entire time.

I was sure, even though she didn't want to admit it, she was nervous about migrating again. I felt like I could fly a million miles and not rest or eat once as I watched Alaska move and change underneath me.

Once we arrived, everyone scrambled to feed on the fresh grass and the mother geese searched for suitable nest sites for this year's chicks. I was so relieved to be home again and eating fresh plant matter again. Even the breeze seemed to welcome me home to the place I was hatched. I waddled slowly to my nest and saw my parents already there. Mother and Father were fixing the nest up for this year's chicks.

"Hey!" I honked to Mother.

"Oh! Hello, my gosling," she answered. She picked a bundle of feathers from underneath her wing and set it carefully in the center of the nest where she would lay her eggs.

"Can I help?" I asked.

"Sure," She answered. "Bring some young, soft reeds and you can practice placing them in the nest." I waddled to the water and found the tall plants growing by the water and carried them back to Mother. Father must have left for more grass, because Mother was with some of the other chicks on the nest who had just arrived. She slowly dropped herself down onto the pile of natural materials and shaped it so that she was comfortable. When she saw me, she honked and opened her beak. I gave her the grasses and she placed them in the nest.

Then, I heard a honk behind me as Eiloo landed on the thawing ground. "Tuah!" he said cheerfully.

"Eiloo!" I answered.

"Did you and Lexa get back okay?"

"Yes. Lexa is helping her parents with their nest," I answered.

"When will they hatch?" Amava asked Mother.

"Twenty-five days," Mother answered. She had just finished laying the last egg yesterday when Mother and Father arrived. We were all peering down at the little white creations. It was so amazing to imagine what was inside of them. Tiny little beings that would soon emerge and see the world for the first time. Mother had told us how we had looked just like the eggs underneath her now.

"Can we help name them?" Suma asked eagerly.

"Most definitely," Mother answered, bursting with pride. Father was standing beside Mother, a limited figure in my life.

He was essential to the survival of these chicks and was with my clutch, too, although I never had a good relationship with my father, I thought. I had seen Heru and some of my older siblings with him before, but I hardly ever spoke to him in my life. As much as I wanted to be like him, we just didn't seem to fit together. He was quiet, deep, and protective and I was young-at-heart and shy. And incompetent. And weak.

Would I ever be like my father? The goal had seemed so easy as a chick, but now it seemed far out of my reach. My teenage years brought these kinds of thoughts that didn't fade when I became an adult. I didn't hear the names that my family agreed on. I sipped marsh water from the same place I had first touched water. I must have looked and acted so different. I didn't miss my chickhood. I was so glad that I didn't have to struggle with survival as much now.

- CHAPTER 11 -

THE SUN BROUGHT A beautiful morning with it the next day. I woke up from my spot on the moist grass and preened with some of the dew that had gathered on my feathers. I walked down to the water and plucked some of the grass from the bank. After eating, I brought Lexa some berries as I usually did and she thanked me graciously and told me to stop wasting my time bringing them to her. I always ignored her with a smile when she said that.

"How are the eggs in your parent's nest?" she asked.

"Good. I don't have much to do with them. Everyone else is always surrounding them and talking to them and I am just fine to watch."

She nodded. "I'm one of the geese that are always with them and talking to them the way you describe your brothers and sisters. I'm so excited for them to hatch! Oh, Tuah, just imagine the little bundles of wonder tumbling around and tripping over their little feet!" she said.

"So, you'll want some of your own next year," I said.

"Of course!"

I didn't understand how much she loved the chicks. They only made me thoughtful of my own life, and what happened when I was a chick.

"Lexa, Lexa!" someone honked, bursting through the reeds next to us. It was one of Lexa's sisters. She was mostly grey and had very little white on her neck and tail. She looked a little younger than Lexa and me.

"What is it, Vila?" Lexa asked.

"The first chick of the colony has hatched!"

"Hurry, Tuah! Everyone will be there seeing the chick!" Lexa honked.

I reluctantly followed her to the nest where the first chick was. Lexa flew, but I couldn't pass up the excuse to fly. We dropped down in the middle of the crowds of geese around the nest and Lexa slipped through the other geese. I pushed through weakly and saw the chick.

Suddenly, I was taken aback by the look of it. It was curled up with its shell next to it. It wasn't fluffy, its down was flat on its small body and there was a small, flat mark on its beak where the egg tooth was. It looked so innocent and untouched by anything in the world. His little feet were pressed against his body, still in the position they were in when he was in the egg.

"What's his name?" someone asked. I snapped back to reality to hear all the questions that were being asked to the mother and father.

"Whilu," the mother answered sweetly.

"Whilu," I whispered to myself, along with a few other geese.

The little body was only moving when he breathed as he was curled up next to his mother. I finally realized why Lexa and everyone were so excited about the chicks. I simply couldn't understand why anyone could not completely adore this little chick.

Other geese pushed past me as they struggled for a glimpse of the first goose hatched of the year. I slipped away, the memory of the chaste little being still lingering in my mind.

I was actually excited to see the new chicks hatch in our nest. A few weeks later, we were all circled around the nest with Mother slowly standing up to check. She rolled the first egg over and saw no peck at the shell. She gingerly moved the next three and when she rolled over the fourth, we saw a small peck mark and the tip of a beak was present in the middle.

"Whoo hoo!" we all cheered.

"Finally!" One of the girls said.

"I can't believe it's hatching!"

Mother peered at the little beak and Father leaned over to look at it. "Hurry, little one!" Suma said.

"Give him time, Suma," Eiloo honked.

"What was that one's name?" Heru asked.

"We named him Parus in honor of her," Mother answered.

The same thing happened to all the other chicks except for three. I asked Father what he was doing a few days later when he picked up an egg with his beak and started to carry it away from the nest. He set the egg down to talk to me.

"This one's a dud," he answered in his low and rarely used voice.

"Oh," I said somberly.

"It's my job to get rid of the bad ones. It will be yours one day."

"Is it hard to be a father goose?" I asked shyly before he could pick up the egg and walk away. He sighed.

"When you are defending your clutch and mate from danger,

yes. Not only your life is on the line, but everything else's life that you love is in danger. Throwing away dead eggs isn't difficult when you don't accidentally crack it. You might see your baby in it that didn't make it, and that takes time to get over. Those are the hardest things to do," he answered coldly as if he had seen that so much that it didn't bother him anymore.

He walked away, and I stood there, frozen. I was horrified. I was now thankful for my shyness that kept me away from my father. Could I bring myself to do the deed that he has had to do for years? Once again, the feeling of inferiority returned and I felt that I was not cut out to be what I wanted to be.

Once the chicks that had hatched were all fluffed up and could walk, we took them to the water. Amava and Suma fought over who would sit on the last two eggs while we left, and being older, Suma won. She proudly sat down with Mother's careful guidance on how to sit on the nest and curled her neck in an s shape. She was giddy with excitement to be able to sit on the eggs.

I now had a job on the water. I was supposed to swim on the left side of the band of chicks and parents. The little fluffs all eagerly hopped in the water and swam with Mother and Father. One of them was especially beautiful, Keinil. She had much lighter plumage than the rest of them and a few dark areas on her feathers instead of being a plain grey like the rest of them. Everyone loved her.

Five chicks on the water. Two eggs in the nest. How picturesque the family looked. Father, with his head held high, Mother, with her caring eyes keeping an eye on all her fluff balls, and the babies gasping at everything they saw. I wished that one day, I could be like Father, and I would finally be able to proudly raise my head at the sight of any other living creature and not try to hide the pride in my eyes.

We soon reached a small island covered in reeds emerging from the ground. Father slipped through the green stalks and Mother followed with the chicks chirping alongside them. I climbed up too and saw the young and short marsh grasses on the inside. They were greener than the grown ones that almost reached above me, but they showed promise that they too would one day grow up.

The chick's lengthy necks snaked back and forth as they pecked at the young grasses. Mother and Father ate as well, but I stayed alert. I soon saw the berry bush I had first given Lexa a berry from and I remembered her.

"Mother?" I said. Her black eyes faced me.

"Yes, Tuah?"

"I need to go somewhere, I will meet you back at the nest in the evening," I honked.

"Where are you going?" she asked.

"To see a friend." She nodded.

I harvested a berry from the berry bush and took off to Lexa. I found her in the marsh swimming on the brackish water. I smoothly slid onto the water and swam next to her.

"Hello, Tuah," she spoke cheerfully.

I set the berry on the water and the little buoyant thing floated next to her. "Oh, thank you. You know how many times I have told you to stop bringing me berries! I'm going to turn into one!" she giggled.

"At least you won't turn into a dead goose by eating berries every day," I joked. She laughed.

"Have you been busy with the chicks in your family? Three died yesterday in my parent's nest. Fox," she said, her smile fleeing her face.

"Oh no. I'm so sorry," I said sadly.

"It's fine. What are your chick's names again?"

"Keinil, Parus, Ohna, Hawan, and Calus," I answered.

"Such pretty names," she remarked. "Any eggs left?"

"Two." Lexa dipped her head to the water and ate the berry I brought her. She sighed.

"Summer is beginning. Shortly, we will migrate again and return to build nests of our own. Were you planning on hatching chicks next year, Tuah?"

"Yes," I answered. "I *want* to be a strong father one day." She chuckled. "But I don't know if I can do it."

"Why not? We have already had this conversation Tuah." she asked.

I sighed as the horrible feeling in the pit of my stomach returned. "I just feel like I won't ever be as good of a father as my father," I answered.

"You will. I know you will. I want to be a mother and watch as my chicks hatch and teach them about the world," Lexa said quietly.

I thought for a moment and the dreaded feeling faded away. "Will you come back to the breeding grounds with me, Lexa?" I asked. "I, I don't necessarily mean raise chicks together, I mean stay with me during migration and when we return," I stuttered.

"Yes," she answered softly. "I will stay with you."

- Chapter 12 -

"HURRY, TUAH!" EILOO YELLED. I flew up to the nest as fast as I could to see the two eggs hatching. Suma had moved off the nest and Mother was cradling the eggs. We sat and watched for hours waiting for the chicks to appear. Everyone jumped and peered at the little things every time they moved or pecked at the egg again. I became bored after a while. The sun was beginning to set and I prepared to bed down. I laid down on my little grassy area and the last thing I remembered was the names of the chicks that were hatching, Leimu and Selu.

I didn't dream anything that night. My head was turned around backwards and underneath my wing feathers while I slept. I knew that the chicks would be hatched in the morning and I wasn't willing to stay up all night like Mother and Father and survey their hatching. I awoke to the sound of tweeting and talking, but then I heard something much worse -- sad words were being said. I opened my eyes and walked over to the nest.

I looked down at the chicks that had fluffed up overnight and were now sitting in little bundles before us. "What happened?" I asked.

"Spraddle leg," Mother said sadly. Leimu was happily walking around with the other chicks and infrequently taking a tumble but Selu was struggling to stand up, let alone walk.

"What's spraddle leg?" Parus asked. She was standing next to Mother with the other chicks that had already hatched.

"It's when one or both of a chick's legs point out to the side and make walking difficult or impossible," Father remarked.

"Was it my fault?" Suma asked anxiously.

"I don't know," Mother said. "It can be caused by a vitamin deficiency or having insufficient moisture during incubation or too high of an incubation temperature I think."

"Can we fix it?" Eiloo honked.

"No," Mother answered somberly.

"Will she die?" I asked. Mother looked up at me and I knew her answer. I looked back down at the chick. She was struggling to stand but her legs were weak and she could never stand up for more than a few seconds without falling. Eventually, she laid down underneath Mother and cheeped quietly.

"I will take care of her," I volunteered. "If she can't follow everyone else around I can stay here at the nest and teach her what to eat and how to eat. I can get her to the water so she can have a drink and bring her back up here."

"No," Mother said. "We need you to help protect the others and there is no sense in just trying to keep her alive when she won't be able to survive. She won't have you forever and the moment she doesn't, she will die. She'll stay in the nest when we leave for the water and if sibling rivalry doesn't kill her first, she won't survive winter. I will not let you waste your time and energy on her. I am sorry to sound harsh but that is just the way it has to be," Mother finished sternly.

I was surprised by how mean she sounded. I looked down at

the little fluff ball again. It was so sad that she wouldn't survive. She reminded me of myself so much, and I almost couldn't bear to leave her to visit Lexa.

"What?" Lexa asked worriedly. I told her about Selu, not even attempting to hide the somber tone in my voice.

"The chick, she..." I struggled to say. I shakily sighed, exasperated with myself for not being able to say the horrible words to Lexa.

"What is it, Tuah?" she asked calmly.

"Spraddle leg," I quickly said.

"Bad?" she asked. I nodded. "It happens to the best of them, Tuah. And, I understand why it would affect you so much because of what happened to you last year, but that's just nature."

"How can you say it like that? You, being the one who wants to care for chicks can say that it is fine when one is going to die before it is a season old? This is my chance to prove to myself that I can be a good father or big brother!" I said with an irritated manner in my voice.

"Tuah, you know most chicks don't survive past their first year. You learned that with Parus; just know that it could have well been you who didn't make it to the wintering grounds. The one chick in the nest, the youngest I'll note, that almost didn't survive. I may have played a part in that but it was mostly you who stayed strong. I think you deserved to make it to the wintering grounds or else I would have been one of those chicks that died in their first year too. If you would have died, I would have owed you a debt I would never get to repay," she said.

I immediately felt better. "Thank you, Lexa. Not just for telling me this, but for being there for me even though I told you to leave me," I replied.

"And thank you for saving me," she answered. We smiled at each other and I mostly let go of the idea of saving Selu.

I returned home to see Father walking away from the nest with the last egg in his beak. As I watched him waddle away with the egg, I remembered our conversation. I decided not to talk to him, so I walked over to Mother. She was repairing the nest and preparing it for the chicks to return. They were playing in the reeds and Selu was sitting in the grasses watching the others defeatedly. She didn't try to move, but just sat there silently. I couldn't bear to look at her anymore, and I turned away.

"Jaeger!" a goose honked from somewhere in the marsh. The nearby geese honked their warning calls and screamed for their chicks to come. My head swung back around and I saw the bird gliding over the colony searching for the perfect weak chick- Selu.

"Chicks, come!" I yelled to them. Their heads perked up and they hastily hopped back to Mother and hid under her.

"Hurry, into the reeds!" she whispered. Mother called a warning call to my father and he came flying over. Eiloo was the only other bird around and he flew in with Father.

"Where is Parus when we need her to get revenge on the Jaeger?" Eiloo asked me jokingly.

"Let's get revenge for her," I answered.

"Yeah," Eiloo answered. The bird had a grey back with black primary wing feathers and a tail like a goose's but with two long, tapered feathers hanging off the tail that whipped around when he flew. He had a mostly white underside and a wide necklace of white feathers. His black shining eyes studied us sharply. Suddenly, he dove and I didn't notice that Selu was still on the reeds struggling to follow after Mother and had gotten stuck upside down. Her little feet kicked and she flapped her little wings as she tried to right herself. I knew that a jeager could still do a lot of damage to a second-year goose, but I couldn't resist trying to save her.

"Selu!" I screamed as I flew towards her.

"Tuah, no!" Father called after me.

"Stop him, Eiloo!"

"Wait, Tuah!" Eiloo yelled. He had flown from higher on the hill and had more speed. Eiloo slammed into my side before I could reach Selu.

"Get off, Eiloo!" I honked helplessly. Eiloo was bigger than me and I couldn't get out of his grip. The jaeger flew down and easily plucked Selu from the ground and took off with her in his claws.

"Tuah! Mother!" she screamed from the sky.

"Selu!" I honked powerlessly. "Sister," I cried.

The jeager happily glided away with a meal for his chicks and I watched him until he disappeared on the horizon. Eiloo let me go when the jaeger was too far away to reach. I was fuming with anger. "I could have saved her!" I protested to my father.

"You could have put all of the other chicks in danger! She wasn't going to survive anyway!" he yelled harshly at me.

I turned to Eiloo. "What was that you said about getting revenge on the jaeger?"

"I didn't mean putting the rest of us and Mother and the chicks in danger."

Mother emerged from the reeds with the rest of the chicks. "How could you let him take her away?" I asked her.

"It took all I had," she answered honestly. "But I knew that it was nature's plan."

I stared in disbelief at my family. I looked at my father angrily. "I hope you know how much I look up to you. I have spent my entire life aspiring to be like you and you just set such a bad example by letting her go," I said to him.

"If you want to be like me you will do what I ask of you!"

After a moment of silence Eiloo said, "Tuah, don't try to be the hero anymore."

I gasped at the words my brother said. In a way, he said it to protect me, but the words he used struck me severely. I never tried to be the hero, I just wanted to keep what I loved alive. All my problems and inferiorities suddenly flooded back to me. I couldn't get another word out of my mouth, so I left.

I turned and took off into the sky, not knowing where I was going. Then I remembered something from the wintering grounds. I knew where I would go. There was nothing left for me here and I knew that I would never become a successful father being the way I was. I took death too harshly and I didn't weigh loss and gain. I loved what I had so much that losing them almost killed me. I had to leave this place. One place in the world seemed to suit just fine – Canada.

- CHAPTER 13 -

I FLEW TO LEXA to tell her goodbye-I couldn't leave without seeing her one more time. I discovered her pecking at the grass and eating her midday meal. It took everything I had to make myself walk to her as she looked up at me. "Back so soon?" she asked.

"I'm leaving."

Her smile turned to a face of shock and horror and I regretted that I had told her so straight forward and fast. "Wha-," she stammered. "Why are you..." Then, her face turned to anger and hurt. "You asked me this morning if I would stay with you and I said yes. Was that a trick? Are you really breaking your promise?"

I quickly remembered the promise and regretted that I had asked her that too. "Why?" she asked unkindly.

I looked down angrily as I remembered. "A jaeger attacked the chicks. Mother hid with most of them but Selu didn't make it into the brush fast enough. I ran to save her but Eiloo held me down. Mother, Father, Eiloo, and I watched as the jaeger took Selu and flew away with her. I was outraged with my family and they were shocked with me. I have to leave them. I'm going to Canada to live with the Canadian geese. I can't go back home." I took a shaky breath. "I can't be a father," I said.

"You would leave me?" she asked coldly and painfully.

"I came to say goodbye." I was beginning to dread leaving Lexa and the promise I had given her.

"I thought you loved me," she whispered, her beautiful voice cracking. "Why else would you ask me to stay with you?" I looked down shamefully. Maybe I had made the wrong decision to leave. "I love you, Tuah. I always have. Tuah, before you leave, answer one question. *Do* you love me?"

I sighed unsurely. But Lexa stood before me strongly, demanding to know her answer. I didn't realize what love was until I met her. I was now angry at myself for upsetting her and I felt disconnected from her at that moment. She was another goose and I didn't recognize this side of her. If I left, I would lose her too, and it is already evident that I wouldn't take that lightly. I was simply lost for words because I was without an answer. She still stood there, waiting.

Then, I remembered what love was and everything we had been through together. I remembered how I had defended her from an eagle, how she had stayed with me, how we had grown closer in the wintering grounds and how we both remarkably survived. I remembered coming to her territory every day to bring her a berry and I remembered the first time I met her. I had given her a berry. Was that love? Did I love her all this time but not know it?

"Tuah," she said, pleading for an answer. I could tell her patience was waning and my window of opportunity was fading as well. A lump slowly formed in my throat and tears filled my eyes. Acid stung at my throat and the lump grew closer to my mouth as a tear-filled wail, but I swallowed it and spoke.

"Yes, I do love you." I finally answered. "But I can't stay here," I said, swallowing more tears. I started to walk away and she ran in ran in front of me and I stopped. We looked deeply into each other's eyes and for a moment everything paused, motionless. I couldn't smell the saltiness of the marsh or hear the bustle of the other geese in the distance. I couldn't see the lovely green of the tidal grasses or the blue Alaskan sky. All I saw was her. All I saw were her grey and black dotted feathers. Then, she leaned forward and kissed me, and I once again remembered what love was.

When she pulled her head back, she whispered, "Stay with me, Tuah."

I looked into her eyes and thought for a minute. Stay with her or leave and honor my pride. Stay strong for her or leave and attempt to start a new life by myself. The answer was suddenly clear. "I will, Lexa."

There was no hope of me leaving now. I stayed with Lexa the rest of the day and through the night. I couldn't face my parents or family or the shame of not being a good role model for the new chicks until we had all had time to sleep on it. Lexa tried to reason with me that I shouldn't have listened to Eiloo and what he said, and that I was more caring than any of the other geese in the colony. With the image of my family's shock still fresh in my mind, I couldn't agree with her yet. I was reminded of the winter here before we migrated that night. How we struggled to grasp the little bit of body heat we survived off just a little longer by nestling next to each other through the dark and freezing nights. We were together again, but this night held the warmth of summer and the scent of the marsh.

"Wake up, Tuah." Lexa gently nudged me when morning arrived. I slightly opened my eyes but closed them again when the bright summer sun stung them.

"How late is it?"

"Three hours to midday, maybe. Come on, you need to go back to your family."

"I'm dreading that," I moaned.

"There's no way to escape it," she honked. I heard small birds tweeting around me and the usual sounds of the other geese honking in the colony. I saw a few chicks running around in the marshland and winced as I remembered the day before.

I stood up and ruffled my grey feathers. I followed Lexa out of the place hidden in the grasses where she slept and into an open area where we could fly. She took off into the sky towards my parent's nest and I followed her on the windy currents of the sky.

The goslings had all gotten bigger since the day they had hatched and it surprised me how fast they had all grown. We glided over the water where I first swam and landed on the bank near my nest. Lexa led me to my mother who was sitting on the nest with the chicks underneath her and my father eating near the nest. "You are Lexa, right?" Mother asked.

"Yes. I've brought runaway Tuah back," Lexa joked.

Mother looked at me. "I'm glad you're back, Tuah. We were worried about you."

I could tell that she truly meant she was worried. Father reached the nest and he gazed at me. I made eye contact with him once and he looked away. I guess I was never meant to be close to him.

"Well, I'm going back to my family's nest." Lexa turned around. "Goodbye, Tuah."

"Bye, Lexa."

She gave me a 'good luck' look and flew back to her nest. Father sighed and walked back to what he was doing without even acknowledging me. He seemed a lot older now.

"I'm sorry, Tuah," Mother whispered so that the chicks underneath her wouldn't hear her. "Just give him time."

"Oh, he'll get plenty of time." That wasn't the answer Mother had wanted and she looked down. I didn't talk to Eiloo for a while, but I talked to my other brothers and sisters about it and they told Eiloo what I said. Eventually, I started to talk to Eiloo again and we rebuilt our relationship, but Father and I never seemed to agree on anything and we eventually stopped discussing it.

- CHAPTER 14 -

SUMMER LOST ITS GRIP on the land and Autumn took over once again. The chicks in the nest were almost adult size and they gathered with the other young geese to be warned by the elder goose of humans while the grass finished turning brown. I wasn't planning on seeing the grass be covered in frost, snow, and finally ice this winter. Food became scarcer and when the first snow flurries glided down from the sky, we were ready to flee.

Everything suddenly seemed to move in slow motion. It was my first time actually witnessing the grandeur of migration from the breeding grounds. We were one connected flock, zugunruhe causing our hearts to race with adrenaline and anxiousness.

Zugunruhe is a time when the Earth signals migrating birds that the time to fly has come. I felt it flowing through my veins. It lived in the colony with us, welcomed as one of our own. Suddenly, everything changed. It was like a dam breaking, unexpected and scary. It was a burst of freedom. We all changed. One second ago, we were grey and white bodies on the ground. Calm-seeming geese. The next moment, we were thousands of souls lurching for freedom. Clouds of geese flooded into the sky as the age-old ritual began. Bodies exploded with feathers spread, ready to follow the pull of the Earth as it turned and cooled Alaska.

When it was my turn to go, all I saw was grey feathers and slits of sky between the other geese. As hectic and crazy as it was, I felt at home and safe. This was meant to be. This was instinct. This was freedom. I was free. Something seemed to fuel my tired wings throughout the long journey. It was a certainty that I knew what I was doing. It was like following the rules in a rulebook -- it became second nature. We all traveled together in v-shaped formations across the vast landscape of Alaskan forests and I was proud to be an Emperor Goose.

Just as I had promised, I was with Lexa the entire migration period to the wintering grounds. The cold was less ruthless this year and the winds were weaker. We had no trouble getting to the wintering grounds and there were very few geese who died during or right before migration. We landed on the wet, black rocks as the ocean continued to heave itself into the rocks, still trying to dislodge them. Everyone hastily pecked algae from the rocks or taught the young ones how to open clams and mussels. I heard that Heru and Suma had finally left Mother and Father and began their completely independent lives.

That just left Eiloo, Amava, and me in our clutch that still stayed with our parents. They were beginning to urge us to leave and we knew that when we got back to the breeding grounds next year, they would not welcome us to their nest again.

Lexa and I were together every minute in the wintering grounds. I would bring her food even when she didn't ask for it and I would always open her clams and mussels for her. We would sit together on my favorite rock and watch as the ocean rolled and tumbled unendingly and misted us with salty sea water. The sun managed to keep the water from freezing on our feathers, but we kept each other warm when it wasn't there.

I never seemed to rebuild the relationship with Father because he disagreed on how to be a father. We both knew that nature would take what it needed, but I wanted to protect the ones I loved as best as I could. I didn't know which one of us was right or which was better for the world, but at least now I was old enough to understand our differences. His traditional mindset differed from mine in many ways, but I was beginning to accept his unacceptance of me.

But how do you be a father? Is being a father like being a mother and loving your offspring -- whether they are children or chicks -- unconditionally loving them and protecting them with motherly love? Or is it providing for them and protecting them like a father should?

I must have been a mother in a father's feathers because I acted more like a mother, but I still didn't distinguish between letting something die and it accidentally dying. Loss was still the same thing to me, be it an expected or unexpected. Then I would remember Selu. Some nights I would ask myself, 'What have I done? I almost killed my younger brothers and sisters.' Other nights I would think, 'What is the matter with them? They let Selu die! I could have saved her!'

But, could I have saved her? Could I have fatally injured myself? Should I just try to let it go? It seemed that every trip to the wintering grounds was miserable and not because of the cold, because I felt like I had lost my Father. But I never felt too alone because I had Lexa.

But maybe being a father just depends on the individual carrying it out. Maybe when I returned to the breeding grounds, I could find a middle ground and find peace. I was much older now than I was only a year ago. And Lexa would be there to guide me like she always has. Maybe I could just try to forget about Parus and Selu and the father I loved but wanted more from. And maybe I could let go of my incompetence from my youth. I was almost an adult anyway. What if I just hoped that the summer breeze would allow me to let go of all the things I wanted back and wished I had?

- Chapter 15 -

WINTER PASSED SLOWLY AND I finally grew my adult breeding season feathers. The whites that had been stained brown by the marsh became the perfect white again. My tail astounded me every time I looked at it because of its flawlessness. My wings and body looked like beautiful small rocks in a black and white picture that had turned into feathers in a beautiful pattern. I changed with the other adults and watched the Snow geese that had come change as well. They were all white but had black wingtips that gave their white bodies a handsome ornament.

The weather warmed and instinct brought us back home. We flew over the Pacific together and watched the world move underneath us. The Snow Geese continued farther North and we stopped at our breeding grounds. Lexa and I landed together on the grass that was waking up again and the cool marsh water that was warming. We ate a little and Lexa claimed a nest site. The time we had spent together all our lives seemed to have decided for us that we would not only return to the breeding grounds together but spend the rest of our lives together as well.

She picked exactly where the nest would be and we gathered grasses together and wove them into a nest on the ground. Lexa and I plucked feathers from underneath our wings and placed them carefully in the bowl of the nest along with other soft mosses. She gathered berries and positioned them in perfect spots as decorations for the nest. We worked together harmoniously and it felt like we were building a life together as we formed a small depression in the Earth. The small hill we had placed it on had the most amazing view of the marsh, and I marveled in the beauty of our home. Life was returning and the little patches of snow that were left were fading. I looked down at the nest when we had finished and was proud to call it my own. It was a complete piece of love.

The sun set over the nest and cast shadows of the other geese and their newly created or refurbished nests. The orange light made the land look like heaven, but not because of the sunset, because it was home and it had the ones I loved in it. If I was alone, home would be nothing more than a strange land that I had never laid eyes on before. Lexa stayed at the nest that evening while I left to find Eiloo and see how he was doing. It took me a while to find him, but I recognized him promptly.

"Eiloo?" I asked when I landed next to his nest.

He looked up from his newly finished nest. "Hey, Tuah!" he said happily. His nest was hidden deep in the reeds and was in a safe, shadowy place.

"The nest looks great," I commented.

"Thanks, oh, and this is Edel," he said pointing at his mate with his beak. She looked up and dipped her head at me. She was a beautiful emperor goose with white spots dotted on her wing feathers. I dipped my head back in response.

"How's Lexa?" he asked.

"She's great. I'll hope to see your chicks soon; would it be fine if I brought mine over when they hatch to meet yours?"

"Definitely. Does that sound good, Edel?" he asked.

"That sounds wonderful. It will be good for them to meet their cousins."

"Well, goodnight, Eiloo and Edel. Lexa's waiting for me to get home. I'm glad you two got back safe." I said.

"Bye, Tuah."

I returned home to Lexa and laid next to her in the darkening Alaskan breeding grounds. The last of the sunlight was still slightly visible as the first stars appeared. I closed my eyes and imagined Parus in the stars. I smiled remembering her and imagining her sailing the starry sky with the other dead geese. "You are free now, Parus," I whispered, with tears flowing to my eyes. Her star moved across the sky with Selu's and they danced together, weaving around the other stars and circling the moon. As the sun faded, more and more geese seemed to appear and lit the sky with their happy memories of life and love.

I thought about our return to the breeding grounds. Everything seemed to have changed. I changed. When I thought back to building the nest and remembered everything that just happened, it was all frenzied and blurred together like it wasn't even me doing everything. Have I finally let go and become who I am supposed to be?

"Goodnight, Tuah," Lexa whispered to me, resting her head on me. I leaned against her.

"Goodnight, Lexa," I answered, my eyes still looking up at the sky.

Two weeks later, Lexa laid seven eggs. She carefully stepped off the nest so that I could have a look at them. Her belly feathers brushed over the pure white eggs that lacked the rich honey-colored stain the marsh placed on all eggs. I couldn't have imagined finally seeing my own eggs. Suddenly I realized that my whole world just changed.

"They're wonderful," I whispered when I saw them.

"You are a father goose now, Tuah. Do you still feel like you could not be a good father?"

"Not really. I feel like I have changed."

"Great! Now we get to name them! I've waited my whole life for this!" Lexa said, squeezing in a giddy happiness. She ruffed her feathers happily.

"That one will be Eiloo," I said pointing to one of the eggs.

"And I want her to be Tyto," Lexa said gently nudging another one of the eggs with her beak.

"Do you want to name half of them?" I asked.

"You can't split seven in half, Tuah! You can just pick some of the names that I decided on and you can name the rest your names."

After a while, we agreed on names for all the eggs. We looked lovingly at them. They were arranged perfectly in the nest, each of them with their own little dent in the ground with flattened grasses and moist dirt. They were beautiful white little things sitting together in our nest. I thought at one point in my life I would never be a father goose, but I am. And I was proud of it. I had everything I would ever need. I smiled at the heavenly things with an indescribable feeling or joy within me. I never once thought about how to be a father for a long time. I was one and there was no need to worry about anything else.

I knew that I would protect them with my life, even before they hatched and could hear my voice talking to Lexa or see me in the distance, alert for danger. I was finally what I had always wanted to be.

I guarded Lexa for the following weeks until the eggs hatched. She was on them almost the entire time, incubating them. I would bring her food whenever she needed it, and I drove off other geese when they came too close. Everything moved so fast and time seemed to be in such a hurry, life felt like a dream.

The warm air brought lots of offspring that year and many geese copied Lexa and me on the nests. The mothers, old and new, laid carefully on the eggs and tucked their orange legs securely around our species' future. Down drifted on the wind, castaways from the feathered nests. Fatherly eyes darted everywhere and investigated everything they saw with fresh responsibility on their mind- predators were everywhere and prowled around the colony in search of the weak and vulnerable.

The bustle and honking of the crowded colony soothed me and made me feel at home, like the noise of a city would comfort someone. The grassy marshlands smelled sweet to me, mixed with the scent of other geese and safety. Even though the eggs were only visible when a mother stood up to take a break, I loved to wonder how many eggs were underneath any particular mother and how much life weighed on any father's shoulders. Nine lives weighed on mine, counting myself.

I stood by Lexa the entire breeding season. I began to wonder if the eggs were ever going to hatch when one day she finally called me and told me one was hatching. I quickly forgot what I was doing and rushed to see the chick. I flapped my wings as I ran across the grassy Alaskan marshland towards the nest and slid to a halt as I reached Lexa. I was bursting with ecstasy as I looked down at the egg. A tiny little black beak was sticking through the egg with the egg tooth still intact. "Who is this?" I asked Lexa to remind me.

"Jounu." I beamed with pride.

We sat together while the chick slowly pecked at the little egg and cracked it bit by bit. We were both restless with anxiousness. We waited and waited, the sun slowly moving across the sky and the world moving around us. Both of us were still as we watched the hatching unfold in front of us. Slowly, every little chip was pecked off and the little wet being laid inside half of the egg and rested. He wasn't particularly pretty, but I loved him as much as Lexa did. The little bit of down he had was pressed up against his body and you could see all his muscles and his bony wings and legs. His eyes were slowly opening and when he shivered from the cold Alaskan air, Lexa took the eggshell and threw it away from the nest. She sat down to keep the chick warm so that he could dry and fluff up. I imagined how he must have felt so comforted from Lexa's soft, warm feathers covering him.

"Wow," I breathed. "Our first chick. Did you see the first chick in the colony that hatched?" she asked.

I shook my head. "I was too busy taking care of you and the eggs." Lexa looked down as her smile faded.

"Tuah," she said quietly.

"What?"

"One of the eggs has died."

"Oh no." I said. Suddenly, I remembered my father telling me about having to carry away eggs that have perished, but I pushed that thought away. I looked back to her.

"I wanted to tell you after this chick hatched so that you wouldn't be sad through the hatching," she said.

"Which one?" I asked. Lexa stood up and pushed one of the eggs away from the nest towards me.

I looked at the egg in the grass and thought about my father again. "My job is to get rid of the bad ones," he had said. "It will be yours one day."

And now it was. I began to remember the feeling that I had felt in my youth. That cold, horrifying vision of myself standing frozen from fear as my father explained the worst part of the breeding season -- dealing with the failures. I looked down at the white egg with a hint of orange-brown from the marsh mud and shivered.

"Tuah, it's not that hard. You need to get rid of it or it'll rot and attract predators." Lexa whispered.

"It's not the carrying part that gets me. It's the thought that it was my fault this egg didn't make it and the fear that maybe I would crack it and be horrified at the dead body that came out," I answered.

"Tuah," Lexa whispered. I looked up at her. "It was a dud. It didn't develop. There is nothing in there."

I knew she was correct; a mother goose is never wrong about her eggs. She had more than a touch of worry for me in her voice, but I heard a new feeling -- fear from not understanding me. I couldn't let her down like this. The egg would start to stink eventually and draw predators near. I had to be a father. Thinking about the struggle I was going through to throw the egg away caused the feeling of failure in my gut to become stronger.

I had to do it. So, I carefully picked the egg up with my beak and started to waddle away with it. I walked for almost ten minutes to reach the edge of the colony where foxes, gulls, and jaegers stood waiting for fathers to bring the dead eggs to them. A fox crouched on the ground with his swift eyes locked on me. A few gulls landed on the ground a little distance from me and jaegers hovered overhead, waiting. I sadly set the egg down and closed my eyes as I pushed it towards the predators with my beak. I quickly flew away. Even though there was nothing in the egg, I couldn't watch them take my baby.

- Chapter 16 -

I RETURNED TO THE nest somberly and peeked underneath Lexa to see if Jounu could walk yet. Seeing him lifted my spirits. He was still resting underneath his mother with his eyes glued shut. "When will the others hatch?" I asked. "I expect these ones to hatch next," she said pointing at some of the eggs after she had lifted one of her wings. Lexa stopped and sighed. "Look at them." She smiled.

"They're so peaceful and perfect," I chuckled. "They won't be so peaceful when they hatch, though. I hope you are ready for some loud and exhausting chicks," I remarked.

She smiled. "That won't matter, at least they'll be ours and that's all that will ever matter," she whispered.

Unexpectedly, I perceived danger nearby. "Lexa," I breathed. She became alert to the danger as well. My head swung around, trying to pinpoint the inkling of a sound. The predator knew she had made a mistake making the sound and silenced herself as best as she could. Lexa and I froze. We waited for what seemed to be an eternity to discover where the danger lurked. Lexa looked at me with fear and concern.

Then, the predator jumped from her shelter in the reeds and grabbed Lexa's tail feathers with her teeth. It was an arctic fox!

Her matted coat rippled as she tore at Lexa's feathers and caused a few to became dislodged. Her ribs were visible and her legs were thin and weak looking, as if they might fail her any moment. It was clear that this animal was starving and willing to risk attacking a fully-grown goose for a nest full of eggs.

Lexa honked the alarm call as loudly as she could while she struggled to slip out of the fox's grasp. I knew she had come for the eggs and would take Lexa if she got the chance. This was my chance to be a father, but my instincts kicked in before the feeling of worry formed in my stomach. I lunged at the fox with the claws on the ends of my webbed feet extended. I grabbed onto the scruff of her neck and sunk my claws into her neck. She let go of Lexa with a yelp and jumped back into the reeds.

Lexa guarded the nest with a hissing voice coming from deep in her throat. I got in-between Lexa and the fox. She slowly stalked around the nest, waiting for her opportunity. Fatigue crept into her eyes and she knew that she had probably cost herself her life.

We stared each other down fiercely. She growled while saliva dripped from her gleaming fangs. Her eyes were on fire and she was ready to kill but knew that she probably wouldn't. I curled my neck in a snake-like way and hissed along with Lexa with my wings outstretched and low to the ground. Her tail sluggishly moved with her sly body and body language told me that she had been defeated. The fox stopped growling and realized that she was wasting time and energy with us and disappeared into the brush. Lexa and I let our feathers fall back down to their normal state and we both breathed a sigh of relief. Our clutch had lived another day.

∽

"Oulah," Lexa whispered. Our second chick was hatching. She was much stronger than Jounu and hatched much faster. She forced the shell apart and squirmed out, ready for her freedom. Jounu watched his sister hatch drowsily, but soon got bored and took a nap. Over the next few days, the rest of the chicks hatched. We would stay up late and watch them and wake up early to care for them. Everything was wonderful, until one morning we woke up and Lexa looked at me with sadness. I cocked my head questioningly and she stood up and pulled a chick out of the nest with her beak. It was Jounu. I looked at him and understood Lexa's expression.

The little grey chick was laying down, unmoving on the marsh grasses. His little black legs were pulled against his body and his webbed toes were clenched together. His eyes were shut and his beak hung open slightly. "What happened?" I asked Lexa.

I realized she was crying when I looked up. She sniffled and said, "I don't know. It was just this morning. He was acting tired yesterday and less alert than usual though."

I sighed. "When I return, we can take the chicks to the water. It's nature, Lexa." Suddenly, her expression changed and she looked at me proudly. Somehow this time, the feeling that I couldn't be as good of a father as mine didn't come. I bent down and picked Jounu up by his neck and his body lightly swayed as I waddled to the edge of the colony. As usual, gulls, jaegers, and foxes stood waiting for their food. I shot them a furious look and laid Jounu carefully on the ground.

"Goodbye, my son," I whispered.

I gazed at the animals lurking in the shelter of the reeds and stood still with my head low. The gulls began to lose their patience and stepped forward. The foxes were wiser than them and stayed hidden and still while the jaegers' wings tired and they landed behind the gulls. I still held my ground, frozen. The gulls squawked at each other in a dialect I did not comprehend and I was glad of that. Gulls are lowly thieves and I would never respect them. The jaegers are aggressive predators with sharp senses and should always be respected, but I would never fear one. Foxes can kill an adult goose, but I was angry enough to fight and kill one singlehandedly. I had fought an eagle before, I could take on a couple of gulls and a fox. The gulls inched closer and the foxes moved restlessly. I knew they were hungry, but I was going to make them wait. I held my head low over Jounu and waited for an ignorant gull to try to grab him from me.

The jaegers walked forward, but the gulls were almost at striking point. I readied my muscles and prepared to attack. The foolish gull nervously moved closer, his wings ready to flap him far away from me at any moment. He stuck his beak close to Jounu then pulled back. I knew I could do it, but I waited for the gull to grab Jounu and I would pounce at just the right time. He quietly squawked and hastily reached his beak towards Jounu's body and grabbed it. Before he could get away, I seized his outstretched wing with my beak and pulled him back towards me.

The gulls squawked up a storm and the jaegers took to the sky while the foxes slipped away. I pinned the bird down with my foot and dug my claws into his chest. He screamed and squawked for help but the others were gone. When my anger had burned itself away, I let him go, wounded but living. I honked angrily into the sky. He would survive and I doubted they would take Jounu now and he could rest there in peace.

I returned home to Lexa and five restless chicks. They were now talking and moving around more than they ever had before and I sat down to listen to them chat and watch them trip over their feet. "Father, Father! Where did you go?" Falu asked.

"I wanted to ask him that!" Sorra asked from next to their mother.

Falu shrugged. "Sorry, Sorra!" he joked.

"Where are the other three?" I asked Lexa.

She smiled and stood up. "Come out young ones," she honked. Oulah, Plowu, and Leyos were napping in the nest. They were younger and were still recovering from hatching from their eggs. Their little black beaks were like perfect little buttons on their grey and fluffy bodies. She nudged them with her beak and their little eyes budged. "Wake up, Father's back," she whispered. A warm feeling filled my chest when she called me Father.

All three of them perked up and struggled to stand up. "Father!" Plowu cheeped.

"Come chicks," I said, leading the way to the water.

Falu and Sorra quickly stumbled after me and Lexa helped the others along. Their tiny little tails swung back and forth restlessly. I pushed through the reeds and slid gracefully into the water. The chicks stopped at the water's edge and watched me swim deeper into the water. "Come back, Father!" they called. "Wait for us!"

Lexa caught up behind them and slid her beak between Falu's legs under his tail and gently tossed him into the water. "Woah!" he screamed as he flew over the water and landed on his side. His fluffy down bobbed him back up and he floated next to me.

"Wow!" he cheeped. "That was cool! You guys have to get in here! The water's weird." He dipped his beak into the water and drank some of it, following my example.

Sorra looked behind her and jumped to the side as Lexa prepared to throw her in as well. She laughed. "You missed me, Mother! I'll go in myself." Sorra slowly waddled into the water like I did.

Lexa walked in as well and floated next to Sorra and Falu. "Come, goslings!" she called. "Or a mink will get you!"

"What's a mink?" they asked as they cocked their heads.

"A little brown animal with tiny ears, a long tail, and razor-sharp teeth that eat goslings!" she answered dramatically. The chicks ran into the water and hid behind Lexa. Leyos climbed on top of her and Oulah hid underneath her wing.

"Come," I said as I paddled down the marsh. I was finally a father and I held my head high and swung it back and forth in search of danger as I remembered the first time I touched water. I looked back happily to see the chicks playing joyfully and Lexa watching them with love.

She looked at me. "We finally made it, Tuah," she said.

"We did." I didn't feel inferior, or that I wasn't good enough. I had become what I wanted to be -- a protective father. Although I did not have a gigantic crowd cheering for me, I felt like it. Every marsh grass that swayed, every goose that looked our way, every cloud that drifted our direction was silently thinking, *Congratulations. You have accomplished your life's goal.* Even the ripples in the water were little smiling faces.

We soon reached a muddy bank and walked a little to reach an area with plenty of fresh baby grasses. I started to pluck the grass and Lexa did too. The chicks watched us for a little and soon caught on. They picked the grasses with us until we were all full. The chicks played around in the water while Lexa and I did some much-needed preening.

When the sun lowered, we returned to the nest and the exhausted chicks fell asleep underneath their mother. The stars had appeared by the time we had bedded down and Lexa and I gazed at them.

"Do you think Jounu is up there?" I asked.

"I believe so," she answered.

I found the North star and pointed at it with my beak. "That one," I swallowed tears, "that one is Parus and the one next to her is Selu."

"That dim one is my mother, she always shined only a little and let the other dim ones shine brighter," Lexa said.

"What happened to her?"

"She didn't return to the breeding grounds this year. My father was devastated," she answered.

"We will be two of those one day."

"One day," Lexa answered.

I tucked my head underneath my wing and fell asleep.

- CHAPTER 17 -

"UP, CHICKS! WAKE UP," I said. They opened their eyes from underneath Lexa. She was still half asleep and I was trying to wake the chicks.

"Why do they have to wake up so early?" Lexa yawned. The sun had just reached the horizon and most of the other animals were still asleep.

"I thought we could bring them to Eiloo and his family today."

Lexa seemed to snap awake. "Oh, yes! We can bring them to my sister's nest tomorrow," she honked.

"Where are we going?" Oulah asked.

"We're going to meet your cousins," I answered.

Lexa preened to make herself look nicer and I helped the chicks clean up a little too. I picked a piece of dead grass from Falu's head as he waddled away. "Come on, come on!" the chicks squeaked.

"Let's go!" Leyos cheeped.

"I wish I could have slept a little longer," Lexa moaned.

"You can stay and sleep if you want," I answered.

"No, I want to see Eiloo and meet his mate."

I led everyone to Eiloo's nest through the thick marsh grass. Spring breezes blew through and cooled my head feathers but left the chicks warmed by the few sun rays that slithered through the tall grass. Large thunderheads rumbled on the horizon and I feared that it would rain soon. The rain water would be colder than the marsh water and chicks are much more susceptible to hypothermia due to only having a light covering of downy feathers.

We would have gotten to Eiloo's nest in less than an hour of flying, but we had to walk with the chicks. We arrived at Eiloo's nest at midday and found him and Edel in the nest with their chicks. "Hello, Eiloo," I said.

He perked up. "Hi, Tuah! I'm glad you came. Our chicks have been so excited to see their uncle and his chicks," he honked.

"Good morning, Tuah," Edel said as she stood up. "Chicks, say hi to your aunt and uncle." The little goslings were a little older than our chicks but they still had egg-shaped bodies.

They looked up at their mother when they saw our chicks. Edel nodded. She was sitting on top of them on the nest and all their little heads were sticking out from underneath her. The chicks climbed out of the nest cautiously. Eiloo only had three chicks, and Lexa and I had five.

"What's your name?" Lexa asked Edel.

"I'm Edel. You've met Eiloo, right?"

"I have. I'm Lexa," she honked. The goslings talked amongst each other and were soon playing joyfully together.

We sat down near the nest. "How have you been?" I asked Eiloo.

"Pretty good overall, we lost five chicks, though."

"How?" I asked, shocked.

"A sandhill crane found them when Eiloo was away from the nest and we were only able to save those three," Edel said gesturing towards her chicks.

"I'm so sorry," Lexa said. "We lost two."

"Sandhill crane attacks are rare," I commented.

"I know, but that's why we have so many," Eiloo sighed.

"What are their names?" Edel asked inquisitively as she looked at the chicks.

"Leyos, Falu, Sorra, Oulah, and Plowu. They sure are wonders," Lexa honked.

"What beautiful names. I just love the name Sorra. My mother's name was Sorra." Edel said.

"Oh, really? Tuah and I had trouble deciding on the names. I'm sure I had hundreds of names that I had my heart set on." Lexa answered. We talked together for a while until it started to rain.

"Oh my," Edel said, looking up at the sky. She obviously was upset that our time together was over.

"Come, goslings! You'll catch a cold!" Lexa called to the chicks. Our chicks ran underneath her and Eiloo's ran underneath Edel. Edel sat down on her chicks and Lexa spread out her wings to keep them dry.

"Thank you for this wonderful visit, Eiloo. Say thank you, chicks," Lexa honked.

"Thank you, Uncle!" they all chirped.

"You're welcome," he answered.

"Goodbye," Eiloo's chicks cheeped. We quickly ran back to our nest in the pouring rain.

It pattered fiercely on the ground and splashed marsh mud everywhere. My legs were covered in mud when we got back and the chicks were almost completely covered in it. My feathers were flattened on my body and made me feel much smaller than usual. The chicks were shaking from the cold and Lexa hurried over to cover them on the nest. They hid underneath her while the rain fell onto her back. Lexa sighed over the driving rain. I sat down next to her and covered her with my wing and we waited and watched as the rain poured down on us. The smell of the marsh was much stronger and the only sound we could hear was the rain.

The summer weather truly was miserable. Our bellies and legs were soaked and when you moved you would hear the squish of the mud underneath. Rain splattered everywhere on the ground and the wind chilled us. The thunder roared and lightning crashed everywhere. The lightning lit up the rain and made it glow as it streamed down and splattered mud everywhere. Marsh grasses swayed and danced in the evening light as the wind slapped them in every direction. Clouds covered the sky and blocked the light from reaching the ground resulting in a seemingly longer evening and darker night. I didn't see how I would be able to sleep well tonight. The grass turned a neon green color when the rain stopped and we knew that it was night when the sky darkened. I unhappily stuck my head underneath my cold wing and pressed my head against my warm body to dry the cold, wet feathers.

It rained on and off throughout the night and we woke up to a red sunrise. Everything was surprisingly calm compared to last night's violence. The light from the sun and the water dripping from the plants was peaceful. I was very dirty though, from the mud being splashed on me all night long and my white neck and head were very brown. I slipped into the water to clean myself off, but it was too late. My white feathers had been stained by the marsh and I now looked like all the other older adults. As I walked back home, I noticed that the ground was less wet in the higher areas, but puddles gathered in the lower places and the marsh swelled with the rainwater.

We brought the chicks to Lexa's sister's nest and had a similar experience to the visit to Eiloo's nest, although it didn't rain. The sun shone hard all day long and by the evening, all the moisture from last night's downpour had evaporated.

The chicks slowly stopped sleeping underneath Lexa, but still snuggled up next to her and their siblings. Their downy fluff became covered by new feathers and their cheeps started to sound more like honks.

I became more worried for them as they grew older because they were straying further and further away from us. Although there were fewer dangers since they were bigger and not easy prey for predators, I still had to be on constant alert for all of us. I couldn't believe how fast the spring and summer had passed and how what I had wanted so badly passed so fast. At least I would have next year to be a father again. The chicks grew bigger over the next few weeks and began to drift farther away from Lexa and me.

We found ourselves alone more and we began to miss the chirping and cheeping of chicks nearby. I occasionally found myself bringing home extra berries and presents for the chicks, only to return to nothing but the memory of them loitering near the nest and hiding underneath Lexa. They would sleep in the nest near us and be gone all day long. I guessed that that was how teenagers acted. Every day, I wished they were still the tiny little chicks they used to be.

The other chicks in the colony grew as well and the entire atmosphere changed. The cute waddling of mini geese flopping around and falling over was gone and they became young adults. Stone colored feathers covered the chicks and the beautiful breeding season plumage of the adults faded. The adults' ages were once again displayed as we lost our breeding season feathers and the age gap between the parents and offspring seemed to grow. There were no chicks running around everywhere and it was much quieter as the parents rested from their long weeks of raising their chicks.

With the responsibility of young chicks lifted off our shoulders, Lexa and I roamed around the breeding grounds together and wasted time like teenagers. We preened each other and filled our bellies with ripe berries every day to prepare for migration. Although winter was near, and the weather was cooling, the chicks still slept farther away from us. I hadn't expected them to leave us so soon. It seemed as if their magnetic force that kept them close to us had gone and they couldn't come within five feet of us. I guess we weren't *cool* enough anymore. Lexa no longer sat on the chicks to shield them from the world, they slept next to us and the nest became just a souvenir of the past.

My marvelous breeding-season plumage was reduced to

greys and brown-stained whites again and I wasn't the striking bird I had become anymore. Lexa and I decided to call the breeding season a success if our chicks made it to the wintering grounds during their first year. We were beginner parents and the chances of all five making it there were slim. Even though they bragged to us about their brand-new feathers and how our feathers were old and weathered, they were still little chicks and still very vulnerable to predators. When I had them near me, I always kept my head held high in search of danger.

I never saw my parents in the breeding grounds and I didn't expect to ever see them again. I still held on to their memory and if I saw them again, I would greet them like old friends. I hoped that one day I would meet my chicks again somewhere in life. The evenings became colder and the chicks moved closer to each other at night to stay warm, but still farther away from us. I would stay up late some nights and look at the stars and imagine Parus flying with all the other geese that had died. I pretended that Parus and Jounu met and Parus took care of him for me. I saw Selu who was now almost a fully-grown goose fly with them in the night sky. I missed all of them dearly. Someday, I would see them again and I would fly with them in the never-ending night sky.

- CHAPTER 18 -

"I'M GOING TO FIGHT a fox one day!" Leyos honked one morning.

"I'd like to see you try," Plowu laughed.

"I will prove it to you that I can!" he said as he pushed Plowu over.

"Ah!" she said as she hit the ground.

I shook my head and rolled my eyes as I continued to eat my breakfast. Lexa had stopped eating and was eyeing them and looking for the chance to intervene. Plowu stood up and attacked Leyos with her claws. She had him pinned to the ground and Leyos rolled over as Plowu fell to the side onto the grass. Leyos happily took Plowu's place and pinned her down.

"All right, stop it," Lexa chimed, but they ignored her.

"Ha ha! I can fight you!" he honked.

"You can fight me but you can't win," Plowu answered. "You won the battle but you can't win the war!"

"We started a war? I thought you were already defeated," Leyos said.

"Stop arguing," I said.

Leyos roughly jumped off Plowu and looked around for a comfortable place to sit down and preen. Plowu started to eat some of the grass but kept her eyes on Leyos.

Lexa lowered her head and continued to graze. I kept my head raised and checked for danger, but the marsh seemed calm and quiet. A breeze rustled the reeds and rustled my feathers like it did every day. I could smell the Autumn air in the wind and knew migration would be soon.

Eiloo brought his chicks to our nest that day and the goslings talked together about migration. I loved to listen to them talk amongst themselves about what they thought the world would look like. It reminded me so much of myself.

When they were little, I would tell them stories of a goose named Mounu who spoke of Canada and Canadian geese. He said that if you are ever lost in life, to fly to Canada and you would be safe until you were ready to return home. I told them about the feeling you feel when you return home from your first trip to the breeding grounds, and how much your life changes when you hatch your first chick, and then your second. Oulah always smiled at that. Ever since Jounu died, Oulah was proud to be the oldest chick, but she still missed her first nest-mate.

No matter where I traveled in life, I would never forget all the memories of the breeding grounds with my family. I wondered every night if Parus, Jounu, and Selu missed their home. I don't think even living in the sky like an albatross could match the home and belonging feeling of where you came from. Why would you need to travel the world if you knew that nowhere would ever be like home?

I would sit in my one special spot where I belonged and where I had sat many different times during the rearing of our chicks and remember how I was feeling or what I was thinking about weeks ago. Sometimes I would recall thinking about what I would feed the chicks the next day. Other times I would be weeping alone remembering my sister, Selu. Lexa's voice talking to me about random things in the evenings with the sound of the chicks playing in the distance rang in my ears.

Oh, how quickly time passes. It seemed only yesterday I was asleep underneath my mother, listening to her gently singing us into slumber. But still, if time travel existed, I would go back in time and save Selu, Parus, Jounu , and Lexa's mother. I would give almost anything to have them here growing older with us.

The chicks seemed to grow so fast, and before long I was taking them to the pre-migration gathering to teach them about humans. The elder goose, a new one, was standing in the middle of the gathering waiting for the last geese to arrive. The ritual was so similar to when I was a chick, I caught myself believing that I was still a chick.

"What are we here for, Father? Besides learning about migration," Falu asked. Sorra heard and looked expectantly at me for an answer with Falu.

"Wait and see, chicks," I answered.

The elder goose started to speak and said almost the same words that the other elder goose had said about migration, but one part caught my attention. She said, "When we return to the breeding grounds next year, choose your nesting sites closer to the center of the colony. Humans have been seen near the outsides of the colony and have even taken eggs this year. Never approach a human. If a human comes near you though, fly. Do not try to save your chicks or eggs, there is nothing you can do for them. There may be a shortage of food because the humans are taking over the breeding grounds, but do not panic. The marshlands have plenty of food and it would take a lot of humans to take over our nesting sites. We will not give in and let them take our home that we have lived in for hundreds of years. On a happier note, the wintering grounds are…" she continued to speak but I wasn't listening anymore.

I gestured for Lexa to move away from the chicks so we could talk. We slipped through the crowds of geese still listening to the elder goose and we stood just outside of the flock. The sun was setting and the night sky was seasoned with stars. "What is it?" she whispered.

"Did you hear what she said?"

"Yes. We'll be fine. If we have to, we can nest closer to the middle of the colony, but I plan on nesting in the same place as this year."

"This is not good, Lexa. Humans kill geese. If they take over the breeding grounds, where will we nest?" I asked.

"Farther north," she answered. I sighed and looked over the edge of the colony, wondering if humans were encroaching closer and closer to our home. "Listen Tuah, relax. Don't worry about it."

She walked back to our chicks and continued to listen to the elder goose. What the elder goose said scared me in a way nothing had ever scared me before. This situation seemed more dire than Lexa was thinking it to be. I stood on edge of the crowd looking at the beautiful breeding grounds I grew up in. I could never let humans destroy our home, but humans are the most dangerous predators of all and they take geese at will. If humans were coming for us, we wouldn't survive.

- CHAPTER 19 -

"NOW FLAP HARDER!" I yelled.

"I can't, Father!" Sorra honked back as she fell down for the tenth time. I landed next to her.

"You have to use everything you have inside you. Your will, your strength, everything."

Sorra was having trouble learning how to fly, but Plowu and Leyos had mastered it. They were gleefully flying around the breeding grounds, strengthening their flying muscles. Lexa was training Falu and he was doing pretty good. Oulah was waiting for my instructions while she watched Sorra.

"My wings aren't strong enough, Father," she whined.

"That's why you have to make them stronger by practicing. Take a break and watch Oulah," I said. "Come on Oulah."

She brushed past Sorra and I heard Sorra whisper, 'good luck.'

"Show me again," I said.

Oulah started to run and spread out her wings. She flapped and slowly gained height as she took off over the marsh. I proudly smiled at her as she turned around and landed roughly in front of me. "Good job! You got it!" I honked.

"Come back, Sorra," she reluctantly walked over to where Oulah and I were. "Did you learn something from watching your sister?" I asked like an eager teacher.

"Yes, Father. I learned that you have to take your time and gain speed before you take off," she quoted me.

I nodded and gestured towards the open area where we were flying. Sorra started off in a slow run and took her sweet time before she jumped into the sky. Before she could turn around, her wings seemed to tire and she slid into the water on her feet. I flew downhill to her.

"My wings aren't strong enough!" she complained.

"You still have time before migration. Work on those wing muscles and we'll try again tomorrow. Try flapping your wings in place on the ground and see how high off the ground you can get. It's a great exercise."

We walked back to Oulah, Lexa, and Falu. "How did he do?" I asked Lexa. She hugged Falu from the side.

"My little gosling is a fully-fledged goose."

"Show me by going and finding your brother and sister," I honked.

Falu ran to the practice area and flew over the marshland with the wisdom and practice of an adult goose. "You taught him well, Lexa."

"He has talent with flying," she answered.

"How did my girls do?"

"Oulah still needs more practice but is doing great. Sorra is going to work on her flying muscles more and we will practice again tomorrow," I answered.

"My wings have never been so tired, Mother," Sorra cried.

"That's because you've never used them before!"

"Sorra is going to be the strongest flier there is," Oulah said.

"Time will tell," Sorra answered glumly. She sat down and rested her head on the grass.

"Hey," I said. "Tomorrow you will do so much better. Trust me."

Falu returned to the nest with Plowu and Leyos at dusk. They landed clumsily on the nest and were laughing with each other.

"What is it?" Oulah asked.

"These two troublemakers wouldn't come home with me. Ended up dragging them back," Falu answered.

Plowu laughed. "You played along too! Don't try to seem like the responsible one."

"At least you are home. Now eat while there's still light," Lexa said. They quickly dropped their heads and ate the grass as fast as they could. They looked like they hadn't eaten all day.

"My babies did so amazing today," Lexa honked.

"We aren't babies anymore!" Plowu said through a mouthful of grass. Blades of short grasses were falling out of her pinkish beak.

"You will always be babies to me," Lexa threw back. This time Plowu continued to eat crazily.

"You all remember what the elder taught you?" I asked. Everyone nodded.

The sun finally dipped below the horizon and the world became dark. The stars came out and my favorite time blossomed, night. "Chicks, remember. When you are migrating and you somehow become lost and can't find your bearings, look to the stars. They will guide you home. Follow Jounu's star to the wintering grounds and follow Parus back to the breeding grounds. You will never be lost if you follow your family," I said.

"I remember Jounu," Sorra said quietly. I looked at her sadly.

"Me too," Falu chimed in.

"I remember he was the first one who hatched. I remember him struggling for hours trying to get out of his egg, but he made it and he didn't give up. Sorra could have used his patience," Oulah said.

Sorra looked down and Lexa hugged her. "Patience is a gift, not everyone can have it."

Everyone tired and fell asleep except for me. I watched my deceased family fly across the sky slowly until I fell into a deep sleep with the rest of my living family.

- CHAPTER 20 -

I WOKE SORRA UP early that morning. "Sorra, wake up," I whispered quietly into her ear.

Her eyes drowsily opened and she looked at me, a little annoyed. "Father, the sun isn't even up yet," she said.

"Stop complaining and get up. You want to fly, don't you?" I asked.

She jumped up. "Yes, I do."

"Then, come with me."

We waddled to the flying area and Sorra took a look around. The sun was barely peeking over the horizon and most of the breeding grounds was still a black pool of darkness. "Isn't it too dark?" she asked.

"If you can start learning to fly at dawn you will be able to fly by dusk," I answered. "Now start flapping in place and warm your muscles up."

She started to flap vigorously but not in any rhythm as a few downy feathers floated away from her. She wasn't able to get off the ground because of her lack of neatness. "Stop, stop!" I yelled.

Sorra jumped back slightly because of my loud voice in the quiet early morning air. She stopped flapping and looked at me, waiting for me to speak. "You have to get into a rhythm, you're flapping is too sloppy," I said. I started to flap in the way I wanted her to and quickly lifted off the ground. I pumped my wings instinctively and watched the browning grass below me ripple.

My wings got into perfect synchronization. My tail spread out as I dropped down and I pulled the feathers in as I flapped again and floated back up for a second. I pulled my wings in and landed on the ground.

"I know, I'm trying!" Sorra whined.

"Well, try again," I sighed.

Her little pink beak shook and her eyes became glossy. She started to flap vigorously again without any rhythm, but after trying for a while her wings synchronized and she lifted off the ground like I did. She landed and caught her breath as she tucked her grey wings next to her body. She smiled and panted.

"Good job," I said. "Now that you are warmed up, let's get flying."

She groaned and I laughed. "Come on!" I said. She stood next to me and took a deep breath. "Now this time give it your all, take your time, and keep your wings in sync," I honked.

We looked over the marsh together. The morning sun cast orange and yellow streaks and dark shadows over the landscape. Fall breezes blew by and rustled the reeds and brushed the grass whilst pushing pink, puffy clouds through the sky. "Are you ready?" I asked.

"I'm ready."

"Go," I honked. She ran through the flying area with her wings outstretched and before she reached the water, she started to flap her wings and took off low over the marsh. Her wings didn't seem to tire this time, but she struggled to stay balanced in the breeze. One of her wings was caught below the breeze and she was pulled down and had to land.

"Try again!" I yelled to her from my high point on the hill. She walk-hopped back up the hill and flew down again but couldn't gain height. "Again!" I yelled. She came back up and tried and tried again until midday. Every time she failed, it seemed so disheartening to her it was like she had died. Slowly, she would gain more height each time, but then was never able to go that high again until I gave her another inspirational talk.

Sorra walked to where I was standing after many attempts, gasping for air. "I can't do it anymore," she panted.

Lexa had walked to us and stood next to me. "At least show me one time," Lexa said in her sweet, motherly voice. Sorra sighed. "Please," Lexa begged.

"Okay," Sorra answered. Lexa grinned, but Sorra did not smile back.

She positioned herself to face to marsh. The sun was now in the middle of the sky and there were no shadows or cool breezes or orange and yellow streaks. She took a deep breath and started to run over the marsh. She gave all her energy and soon took off. Her feet clawed at the ground a couple of times and she struggled to gain height. Her wings flapped perfectly together, as in sync as Lexa and me. She flapped and flapped as hard as she could. I could almost hear Lexa cheering Sorra on in her head. It seemed to take forever for her to get off the ground.

Finally, her webbed foot raked at the yellow-green grass and that gave her the last bit of thrust she needed to get into the sky. "I did it!" she yelled from high in the air as she sailed above.

"Yes!" Lexa breathed.

I took off into the sky and joined her with Lexa behind me. We circled together in a weak thermal, celebrating Sorra's introduction to flight. The rest of the chicks saw us and leaped into the sky as we flew over the marsh. Sorra gasped at the sight of the breeding grounds as she finally flew and gleamed with pride and happiness as the other chicks congratulated her. The sun warmed our backs and I found peace flying over the breeding grounds.

After we had enjoyed our flight, we landed back at the nest and Sorra took a hard-earned break that night. I didn't have the energy to stay up and look at the stars and I soon nodded off with the rest of the family.

A couple of weeks later, it was time to migrate once again. We had all eaten all we could in the time before migration and prepared. We stood next to the nest saying our goodbyes to the breeding grounds and waited for the first geese to take off.

"I'm going to miss the breeding grounds," Oulah said for the tenth time.

"We all are, Oulah," Falu remarked, a little annoyed.

Then, we heard the flutter of large wings taking off near us and we took off with our group and formed our famous v shapes in the sky.

- CHAPTER 21 -

"WE ARE FINALLY MIGRATING!" Leyos said happily.

"We are!" Plowu squeaked.

"Which way do we go?" Sorra asked.

"South," Lexa answered.

"Which way is South?"

"Your instinct tells you," I said.

"Just follow us for now," said Lexa.

We flew over the breeding grounds and soon reached the mighty Pacific. The chicks loved the water like I did when I first learned to fly. The flight was easy and quick for Lexa and me, but the chicks tired quickly. But, they all prevailed and made it to the wintering grounds.

"Wow! Look at all the rocks!" Oulah honked when we landed for the first time in the wintering grounds.

"What do we eat here?" Leyos asked.

"Algae, clams, and mussels. Sometimes seaweed," Lexa answered.

We all filled our bellies and rested from the long migration. I flew to my favorite rock and sat watching the ocean roll. Sorra somehow found me and joined me on the rock. "How do you like the wintering grounds?" I asked.

"It's different. I never expected it to look like this," she answered.

"What did you expect it to look like?"

"Rocky, but I didn't think the rocks would be this big." I nodded.

"Would you like to fly with me?" I asked as a salty breeze rolled off the ocean and brushed our feathers.

"Sure."

I took off over the ocean and Sorra followed. The Pacific was rolling and tumbling as it was every winter. Salty air clung to our feathers as we flew. Water sprayed up at us when two waves collided and we flew through a fleeting mist. The winds over the ocean were as wild as the water was. It blew under our wings and lifted us up, then pulled us down and we fought to stay in the air. We glided up and down over the rolling waves together for the rest of the day and returned to the wintering grounds before dark.

"Where were you guys?" Lexa asked when we returned.

"We went out for a flight to celebrate getting to the wintering grounds," I answered.

She smiled. "We've already bedded down. You two better get to sleep soon or I'll not let you go for celebratory flights anymore."

I chuckled and started to preen as the sun slowly descended and soon dipped below the horizon of the wintering grounds.

We took our time waking up the next morning because everyone was still tired from the migration.

"Have you seen Eiloo?" Lexa groggily asked me.

"I have," Plowu said. "I met with his chicks yesterday."

"Good. I was worried he and his family didn't make it to the wintering grounds."

"Do you know where he lives?" Falu asked.

"I think he and his family live on a small rocky island just past Father's rock," Oulah answered.

"Are his chicks there with him?" asked Falu.

"Yeah," Oulah answered.

"I'll meet you guys there later," Falu said. Oulah and Plowu nodded.

I looked at Lexa questioningly. "What are you guys up to?" Sorra asked.

"Maybe you could meet us at Eiloo's and you'll find out," Plowu answered.

"What?" Leyos asked.

"What's going on?" Lexa asked.

"Yeah, what are you doing?" Leyos honked as he stood up.

"Nothing, Leyos," Oulah said irritably. She kept her head low and her eyes darted to the side guiltily.

"As long as you're not causing trouble," I said.

"Tuah!" Lexa yelled.

"What?" I asked.

"What do you mean, 'as long as they're not causing trouble?' My chicks don't even think about causing trouble!" Lexa said. She stood up too.

"Are you going to tell us what's going on or do I have to ask Eiloo?" I honked.

"Eiloo doesn't know any more than you do, Father," Plowu answered with an attitude I didn't like.

I looked at her angrily and she lowered her head. "It's the truth," Oulah remarked.

"What are you up to?" Lexa was about to burst.

"It doesn't matter. Come on guys," Plowu honked. Plowu, Oulah, and Falu stood up and prepared to take off.

"Where are you going?" Lexa yelled.

"Eiloo's," Falu answered. They took off and flew in the direction of my favorite rock.

My head swung around to Sorra and Leyos. They shook their heads in confusion. Lexa sighed.

"Just let them go. If they do something crazy, we'll hear about it soon enough," I said.

"They've never acted like this before! You need to talk to Eiloo about this and see if he knows anything," Lexa honked. I nodded and rested my head on the cold rocks, already tired of this morning's drama.

- CHAPTER 22 -

THAT EVENING WAS JUST as dramatic. I stayed at home and cleaned up our resting places a little while Lexa searched for food. Sorra and Leyos faithfully returned before dark to the nest, but Falu, Plowu, and Oulah didn't. "Where's everyone else?" I asked them.

"We don't know. We thought they would have arrived here before us... I think they are up to something bad," Leyos answered.

Lexa landed on the hard rocks as Leyos finished talking. "Is everyone ready for bed, Tuah?" she asked.

"Falu, Oulah, and Plowu aren't here."

She pulled her neck back and her eyes opened wide. "It's almost past dark!" she honked.

"Maybe they are at Eiloo's," I said.

"Should we go see?" Sorra asked.

"No, it's too late and the moon isn't full enough to fly at night. You won't be able to see anything," I said.

"Oh, Tuah, what if something happened to them?" Lexa cried.

"All we can do is hope that they come back tomorrow or late tonight. Come on, let's go to bed."

Lexa reluctantly dropped down in her resting place next to me as I preened. Sorra and Leyos laid down and closed their eyes. The sounds of sleeping geese in the colony echoed slightly and bounced off the stones while the ocean tumbled over the rocks and sprayed cool, salty mist everywhere.

"Tuah, I have terrible butterflies in my stomach. I'm so worried about them," Lexa whispered to me in the dark. The stars were shining very brightly tonight.

"There is nothing we can do. All we can do is hope," I whispered back. I was very worried about our chicks, but I didn't show it as much as Lexa did. I tried to forget about them and try to get a little sleep, but it was no use. I was awake late into the night, even until the moon was at its peak.

All of Lexa's worrying had caused her to tire and she had fallen asleep next to me with her head tucked underneath her wing. My pitiful sigh was drowned out by the crashing of the ocean and I closed my eyes and fell into a light sleep.

I awoke early the next morning, ready to start the day. Being awake was better than being in that useless worry-induced half-sleep. I was only torturing myself trying to fall asleep. I tried to quietly slip away to go see Eiloo without waking Lexa, but as soon as I moved some of the rocks, she was up.

Her eyes popped open and her head quickly came out from underneath her wings and she looked at me. "Are you going to find them?" she asked.

"You need to stay here. If we go to Eiloo's and they come back here and we are gone, that will just cause more problems," I answered quietly.

She slowly nodded. "I'm coming with you," she said.

"I just said you need to stay here and you agreed!"

"Then you stay here and wait. I have to go to Eiloo's. I'm so worried about them. Well, why don't we wait here a little bit longer and see if they come back."

I sighed and agreed. She stood up and did her morning stretches. The early morning light shone on all of the rocks and made them glow with a beautiful orange haze and when the ocean sprayed on them and caught the sunlight, it truly looked like heaven.

Lexa and I sat on my rock together enjoying the view over the ocean. Over the years, I had found myself sharing my rock more and more. I could feel Lexa's tension next to me more than I wanted to. "Just let it go, Lexa," I said. She shook her head. "Look, I don't understand either! But we will sooner or later so just breathe."

She took a shaky breath and leaned against me. We waited for a while in a stressful silence. I squinted my eyes at something over the horizon. "Who's that?" I asked. A mist of salt blew past us.

Lexa sat upright and found what I was looking at. "I don't know," she answered. We looked for a while until the goose was recognizable.

"It's Eiloo," I said. I honked at him as he landed on my rock next to us.

"Where are my chicks?" I asked him.

Eiloo was panting. He looked like he had flown very fast. "Where are *my* chicks?" he honked.

"I don't know! I thought mine were with you!" I answered.

"They met with my chicks a few times and I didn't pay much

attention, but then yesterday they said they were going back to you and they haven't come back," Eiloo said.

"Have you seen Sorra and Leyos?" I asked.

"They never came to us. All our chicks are gone."

"Oh, no, Tuah! Where could they have gone? Why would they leave? You don't think something attacked them?" Lexa was yelling frantically.

Edel landed next to Eiloo. "I can't find them… I can't, find," she gasped, still trying to catch her breath.

"Calm down Edel," said Eiloo.

"Take a deep breath. We'll find them." Edel began to breathe deeply and soon was breathing normally. I glanced at Eiloo. I saw doubt in his eyes but didn't draw attention to the lie to Edel.

"We have to figure out where they went or if something attacked them. Did you hear them say anything?" I asked Edel and Eiloo. Eiloo shook his head.

"Oh! Yes, they said something about going somewhere you almost went when you were their age," Edel said to me.

I gasped. "Oh no." I groaned.

"What?" Lexa yelled, officially freaking out.

"They flew to Canada."

"What?" Lexa screamed.

"Why?" Edel honked.

"I almost flew to Canada when I was younger and they must have gotten the idea from me."

"They've never done anything like this before!" Lexa said.

"What do you mean you almost flew to Canada?" Eiloo asked.

"It doesn't matter what happened with me. We need to see if Sorra and Leyos are still here. Come on." I said.

I took off in the direction of where we might find Sorra and Leyos. Thankfully, we saw them floating on the water together.

"What's going on?" Sorra asked, clearly surprised to see all of us.

"Oh, thank goodness," Lexa breathed when she saw them. We landed on the rocky shore. Leyos looked up.

"Come up here!" I yelled from the rocks. They looked at each other, confused, then flew up onto the rocks.

"What?" Sorra asked, shaking her feathers off.

"Where are Eiloo's chicks and Oulah, Plowu, and Falu?" Lexa asked.

"We don't know. We already told you that. Did they leave?" Leyos asked.

"We think they went to Canada," Edel honked.

"Huh?"

"Why?" Leyos asked.

"Maybe for adventure, I don't know, but we need to find them," I said.

"We do?" Leyos said.

"What?" I asked.

"I mean if they left, they will probably come back and I don't see how you could find them. We have no idea where they went. Canada is huge. And if they joined Canadian geese like you told us in your stories, then they could end up migrating into America," Leyos answered.

Eiloo cursed underneath his breath. Lexa sighed, emotion thick in her voice. She sounded on the brink of tears. Edel stayed quiet and thoughtful with her head tipped slightly sideways.

"Are you sure you have no idea where they went?" I asked again.

"They told us nothing, Father!" Sorra yelled.

"Okay, I'm sorry."

"Tuah, they know nothing about Canada. They would have had to ask someone about it. Maybe they talked to someone before they left," Edel said.

"That old goose! What was his name?" Lexa asked, looking at me hopefully.

"Mounu."

"Let's split up. We need to find him as soon as possible so that the they don't get too far," Eiloo honked.

We all took off and started to search for Mounu. Lexa caught the breeze and flew Northwards over the flocks of black, white, and grey geese. I glided slowly, not risking letting Mounu slip through my wingtips. The colony was loud, and I didn't have much hope of us finding him. I flew lower and hovered just over the heads of the geese. I let my legs hang down and my wings pumped vigorously to keep me in the air in this difficult aerial situation. Worry was plenty to fill the hole of evaporating energy within me.

"Please, someone!" I called desperately. "Does anyone know a goose called Mounu?"

Concerned eyes looked up at me, confused, uninterested. Heads shook and eyes darted to the ground, not wanting to be a part of my desperation or hoping that someone else will step up and call out my much-anticipated answer of hope. No matter how loud I honked, the sounds of other geese drowned me out and my voice faded away with sorrow.

I hated myself for thinking irrationally in my youth and I was angry at my chicks for thinking irrationally in their youth. I shook my head with emotions of anger, sadness, and despair swimming through me like a beached fish praying for help and flapping helplessly to no avail. My wings burned like the fire of anger in me and tears gathered in my eyes. I looked up from the ground and suddenly felt so alone and I looked around for something I could recognize, something that I loved that loved me back. All I saw were strangers and a place I was unfamiliar with.

My breathing was as fast as a hummingbird's and my chest ached when I swallowed and my breathing paused. I began to feel dizzy as my head spun around in an endless circle of confusion and misery. Everything became colors mixed together like a soup of reality, but it had soured, molded, and become stale. I swallowed more, straining to rid my mouth of the foul taste of the nightmare. A whine escaped my throat and more tears swirled the soup of the world ever more. Words swirled like the rings of a tree stump in my head -- unfinished, confused, biased, painful. I couldn't feel my wings throbbing in enervation anymore.

Finally, I saw something in the distance. The picture flew to my mouth and the vulgar taste of sadness, anger, and desperation drifted away as the wonderful picture in my mind replaced them. It was my rock next to the ocean that sprayed and splashed the rocks. I stopped spinning and pulled my legs back up underneath my belly feathers and changed the position of my wings to point me to my rock. I flapped harder than I ever had before and everything around me drowned out and all I saw was the rock. It wasn't a particularly big rock, or pretty rock, but it was mine and I needed it.

I flew, unknowing of the time it took me to get there, or the distance I traveled. I forgot about the chicks and Lexa and our search and just flew. I landed with my feet outstretched and my wings catching all the air the ocean blew at me. A spray of salt water cooled me as I felt the burn of my wings when I finally relaxed my muscles. My legs gave way and I sat down. I sighed and closed my eyes as I caught my breath and oxygen flowed to my head and the fog cleared like the sun rids the forest of the morning mist. I looked out over the ocean as I recollected my thoughts.

"You okay, Son?" I heard him ask from behind. I swung around but saw no one behind me. I looked around for Mounu and didn't see him. I had imagined it.

I moaned loudly. "Why would they leave?" I asked myself out loud. I rested my head on my back and hid it underneath my wing feathers. Suddenly, I felt very tired and I didn't think it would hurt to take a quick nap and I let my thoughts drift and my eyelids drop.

- CHAPTER 23 -

"THERE YOU ARE!" someone yelled. I opened my eyes and quickly lifted my head up. The sunlight fired a brigade of arrows that stung my eyes they struggled to see in the bright evening sun. I must have fallen asleep.

"Tuah, Edel found Mounu!" Lexa honked.

"What were you sleeping for?" She landed on the rock next to me.

"I didn't mean to fall asleep. I couldn't find Mounu and I tried to figure out why they had left a-and I, I didn't mean to fall asleep."

"Come on!" she yelled jumping into the air. I stood up, my legs uncertain, and followed her.

"Ah, is that you Tuah? I hardly remember you," he asked when I landed next to Eiloo.

They were standing together on the edge of a rocky shore with snow covering the rocks. The ocean water flowed past the tiny island and melted the snow next to the water and more snow drifted down from the sky softly. Mounu seemed much older and frankly, on the brink of death. His white neck feathers had browned and his body was a dull grey.

"Did you let them leave?" I asked hurtfully, quickly jumping to the point. Edel was standing next to him and was interrogating him when Lexa and I arrived. Mounu was still wet from swimming in the water.

"They just came up to me one day and asked about Canada and how to get there. I told them everything they asked me and then I asked them if their parents knew about this, and they said that you did," Mounu answered.

"They lied?" I asked.

"What?" Lexa asked.

"Where did they go, again?" Edel asked.

"Yukon. It's the closest part of Canada to Alaska. In fact, I know a goose who is friends with a human in Yukon," Mounu remembered, his old mind straying from the point.

"How did they know how to get there?" Eiloo asked.

Mounu snapped back from his thoughts of the human in Yukon. I would become slightly afraid for his health in the future by the way he drifted away occasionally. "They followed a Canadian there named Nau. He is a friend of mine who came back with me when I traveled to Canada. He had been living with Alaskans and was ready to return home. There might be another Canadian here who knows Nau and could take you to their breeding grounds," he answered. "I can find one for you, I am sure there is one here, to make up for letting them leave without asking you first."

"Go, please," I answered impatiently.

Mounu took off in search of a Canadian. His flight pattern was strange and his wings were weathered from years of flying.

"They sure have adventurous spirits to want to go all the way to Canada," Sorra honked.

"They had to have been planning this for a long time," Edel commented.

We waited for a long while before Mounu returned. The sun lowered near the horizon and we wouldn't get too far without flying at night if we took off now. I looked around anxiously, wondering if he would ever come back. We were mostly silent, barely a word muttered between us. I was so tired of waiting. I stood up and shook my feathers angrily. "I can't believe they left!"

"We'll find them, Tuah." Eiloo said. I sighed.

Finally, Mounu landed on a small rock next to us with a Canadian goose next to him. "This is Cuan. She can take you to exactly where Nau flew with your chicks," Mounu honked.

"Hello." Cuan said. We all greeted her, but she seemed ready to leave promptly.

"We better hurry before the sun sets. Follow me," she said taking off into the sky. I cocked my head at her strange accent. It was definitely a northerner's accent but more like a northeastern goose's. We took off behind her in the direction of Yukon. I was slightly nervous of our lack of vision, but I followed Cuan nonetheless.

"So, you're from Canada?" Eiloo asked Cuan.

"Yes, I came to visit Alaska this year and I am very happy to help you find your chicks. I was just about to start my migration back to Yukon too."

"How long will it be?" Leyos asked.

"Oh, not long at all," Cuan honked.

"So what are your chicks names? My brothers and sisters were very eager to explore too."

"Ours are Oulah, Plowu, and Falu," Lexa answered.

"Mine are Dilu, Vula, and Uma," said Eiloo.

"Such pretty Alaskan names. I will name one of my chicks this year Plowu. What are your names?" Cuan asked.

"I am Eiloo and this is Edel," Eiloo said pointing his beak at Edel.

"I'm Sorra."

"And I am Leyos," he added.

"I am Tuah," I honked.

"And I'm Lexa."

"Wonderful. Are you okay with flying by moonlight?" Cuan asked.

We all nodded. I was nervous about it, but it was worth it if we were going to find our chicks. "Good, because the sun is just about to disappear. I love watching sunsets here. I will return to Alaska next year and I may even nest with emperors." Apparently there was a whole breed of geese that had a taste for leaving their homeland.

The last rays of light faded and the moon and stars appeared. The moon was halfway full, but we managed to see enough. The snow glowed in the moonlight and helped us to see the ground better. The stars seemed to glow brighter than they ever had before and truly lit up the sky.

I found Parus, Jounu, and Selu flying together. They faithfully followed us across the sky all night long. "Why are you looking at the stars so much, Tuah?" Eiloo asked as he flew along beside me.

"You see those three bright ones next to each other?" I asked.

"Yeah."

"That's Parus, Jounu, and Selu. Or at least that's what I pretend, to help me cope." I whispered.

"Wow, I never thought I would see Parus again and there she is, high in the night sky like she has been all year," Eiloo honked. "She made our pair a trio and kept us together through all of our fights and arguments. I miss her."

"Me too, Eiloo."

- CHAPTER 24 -

WE WERE STILL FLYING when morning finally arrived. "Good morning everyone! How did you sleep?" Cuan honked when the sun rose.

"We didn't," Leyos said, matter-of-factly, as he stifled a yawn.

"I know! Just making a joke."

"Can we rest? My wings are burning like the sun. I don't think I could keep flapping any longer," Sorra whined.

"Oh, just a little longer. We'll be there by mid-sun."

The landscape changed to mountainous forests and rocky grasslands. By midday, we were looking down on flocks of thousands of Canada geese on the ground with nests and eggs. Snow only dotted the landscape here.

"My, how many Canadians live here?" Edel asked.

"Most of us," Cuan answered.

I saw a huge figure on the ground and recognized what it was. "Human!" I honked in the warning call. Everyone looked down and started to panic except for Cuan.

"Oh, calm down! Many humans live here and attack us. We're all used to it."

"Is that why there is so many of you? Because of the humans? Do you have to keep your population high because they come and kill you?" Leyos asked.

"Sort of. They come every spring and take some of our eggs and kill a few geese throughout the year, but if we sacrifice a few of us, then the population stays healthy."

"I hope our chicks haven't become one of the sacrifices for the humans," Lexa whispered in my ear.

We slowly descended and landed on the ground in the middle of the goose colony. It was very loud and smelled way worse than our colonies in Alaska. The weather was still cold, but I had been colder. There were nests and eggs and geese everywhere and I wondered why anyone would have wanted to come here. Geese hissed viciously at me when I got too close to their nests. Backing away, I would get too close to other nests and they would hiss at me too. It was way too crowded for my taste.

"Welcome to Yukon, Alaskans! I hope you find your chicks. This is where I leave you, I have my own business I have to attend to. Goodbye! And good luck!" Cuan honked at us over the noise.

"Thank you, Cuan!" we honked back to her.

"We wouldn't have made it here without you," Eiloo said.

"Goodbye!" Sorra honked.

"You're welcome." She said as she disappeared into the crowds of geese.

I was already fed up with being hissed at. I was in everyone's way and I hissed back at one of the geese who hissed at me. She stood up on her nest and honked, "Get away!" I saw her eggs underneath her and she was much bigger than me, so I caught up with the rest of my group. The honks and hisses of other geese rang in my ears.

"How are we going to find them?" I asked.

"The flock is too big for us to fly over and find them, so we will have to think of something else," Sorra said.

"And it's way too loud for us to call for them," Eiloo said.

"What? I can't hear you," Lexa honked.

"Let's fly to the edge of the flock so we can hear each other better," I yelled. I heard a loud boom in the direction where I saw the human and the geese in that area took off and abandoned their nests.

"Fly!" Leyos yelled.

We took off and headed over the colony. As I pulled my legs up underneath my belly feathers, I looked down and saw all the Canada geese. A few of them had taken off with us, and until we flew above the others that were flying as well, I became very afraid of the tornado of birds and feathers and fear that we flew in. They looked very different from us. They had mostly brown bodies and black necks with white behind their eyes. They had black beaks and legs, we have orange legs and pink beaks. My neck wasn't its usual brown stained white, I noticed that I had started to grow my breeding season feathers. Once again, I remembered the joy of the breeding season and the beauty that my feathers beheld. The thousands of geese moved around underneath us and I imagined that it would be such a spectacle to watch these birds migrate in these huge flocks.

Slowly we descended and hovered above the ground as we eyed spots to land. The green grass below us was unusual, we were more used to harsh, tough grasses. It was much quieter and calmer here on the edge of the flock and the geese around us calmly rested on their nests.

"Okay, so, we can hear again," Sorra said.

"Yeah," Leyos answered, looking around.

"What are we going to do?" Lexa asked.

We were all silent for a little bit while we waited for someone to come up with an answer or for something to pop into our heads. "Let's eat and rest and then try to decide our next move later," I honked. We hadn't eaten anything for a while and we missed a night of sleep last night. We had begun to look dreary and tired, and I thought this would be the best option for all of us. Everyone agreed, and we found an open area away from the other geese and laid down.

I preened while everyone rested. I couldn't imagine living in such a tight colony and even rearing chicks out here. It was too loud and crowded, and the humans came every day. I much more enjoyed the calmness of the Alaskan wilderness and the crisp spring mornings when the dew gathered on my back. I loved the smell of the marsh and the thought of swimming in it made me homesick. Oh, the beautiful Alaskan morning sun peeking over the mountains and lighting up the fog and reeds as I glide through the marsh, not disturbing the misty air. I noticed that I had closed my eyes as I remembered my home. The sounds of the loud colony filled my ears once again and I wished I was home even more.

I glanced to my side and saw Sorra and Falu curled up next to each other in a deep, calm sleep. Lexa had tucked her head underneath her wing feathers, so I couldn't see if she was asleep or not. Eiloo and Edel were leaning against each other, resting. I couldn't sleep. There was no way I was going to rest when we needed to find our chicks.

I flew over the flock many times and dodged many humans while my family slept. I had never seen so many humans in one place. They carried the sticks the elder had described with them and when they boomed geese fell limp or fell from the sky. The humans didn't seem to mind if they stepped on the Canadian's eggs or nests or even the adult geese. They would kill geese who stood in their way and brushed aside the ones that couldn't get out of their way.

Even though it was a death zone where the humans were, in the other parts of the flock, many more geese thrived and there was a surplus of birds there. It seemed to all be in balance, if you have too many geese, the humans take as they please. Emperor geese are much rarer than Canadian geese and we hardly ever see humans. I imagined our breeding grounds looking like this, with humans everywhere killing what they wanted to. I thought of them splashing through the marsh water that we swim in and pushing over the reeds that we hide in and ran through as chicks.

Then, as my thoughts left my control, I saw Lexa on our nest hissing savagely at a human as it approached her and the eggs underneath her and my last thought being a boom. I shook my head in fear as I glided over the goose flock and banned the thought from my head. I would never let that happen. I would never let humans encroach on our breeding or wintering grounds.

- CHAPTER 25 -

I FLEW BACK TO the group just as they were waking up. "Did you find them, Tuah?" Lexa asked when she saw me return.

I laid down next to her. "No," I answered.

"We'll find them, don't worry," she said.

"It's all my fault. If only I hadn't considered coming here when I was young and told them about it. Then we wouldn't be here at all. We could be in the breeding grounds on a new brood of eggs waiting for them to hatch," I muttered.

"It's not your fault! They are just young and wanted adventure and to see the world. And no one can blame them for that, so don't get too angry at them when we find them, but I will let you get angry at them for not telling us first. And don't be angry at yourself because you didn't cause this!" she honked. Everyone opened their eyes a little.

"Okay," I said, not wanting to continue our conversation further in front of Eiloo, Edel, and our chicks.

Lexa seemed to get the cue, but then she said, "We'll finish this talk later." I sighed.

Once everyone was awake and ready to go, we thought about what we would do next. We gathered together and finished preening as we discussed it.

"What was Mother yelling about, Father?" Leyos quietly asked me.

"Nothing, Leyos."

"She was yelling about something. Mother doesn't yell for no reason."

"You don't need to know, Leyos." I said sternly.

"Maybe we should find Nau because he might know where the chicks are," Clever Edel said.

"Good idea, but how are we going to find him?" Sorra asked.

"We can't just go nest to nest asking if they know a goose named Nau because there are way too many geese," Leyos added.

"Maybe instead of us finding them, we could make them find us," Lexa honked.

"What do you mean?" I asked.

"We get their attention somehow by either spreading the word or drawing attention to ourselves and if they see us, we might be able to find them."

Leyos laughed. "Yeah, let's go attack a human and let that gossip spread through the flock like a disease and at least tell them that we are here."

"It's not worth attacking a human just to get their attention," I said.

"That's not what I meant," Lexa honked. "But we could use a human somehow."

"Hey! Maybe we could get a human to scare all of the geese and get them up into the sky then we will have a better view of finding them because on the ground they can hide, but if they fly up, we will be able to see the difference between six emperor geese and thousands of Canada geese," Sorra said.

"Yes! Their bodies will be grey against the Canadians' brown. Does everyone agree?" I asked.

"It's worth the risk, even if we have to mess with humans," Leyos said.

"Maybe we could get a Canadian to help us. They have more experience with humans than we do," Eiloo commented.

"I agree," Edel honked.

"Me too," Lexa said.

"Who do you think we can ask for help?" I asked.

Sorra scoffed. "Anyone! We have plenty of geese to choose from here."

We heard another boom from the humans and the geese around them flew into the sky. "How about them?" Leyos asked after looking around some.

We looked where he was looking. There was a pair of geese near us on a nest. "Alright. Who is going to ask them if they want to help some Alaskans risk their lives trying to get a human's attention?" I asked. Everyone was quiet. The plan really seemed crazy when you thought of it that way. "Fine, I'll do it." I moaned.

I walked in the direction of the nest. The female looked at me suspiciously and her mate eyed me with a dangerous gaze. I could tell they had eggs or chicks by the way the female was sitting on the nest. When I got close to the nest, she began to hiss quietly. I stopped before I got too close to the nest. "Excuse me, could you help us or do you know anyone who could help us get a human to scare everyone in the flock into the sky?" I asked.

The male goose laughed. "No way are we going near a human, but I know someone who could help you."

"Who?" I asked.

"A goose named Growan. He lives just down that way. He is the perfect insane goose to help you with that insane idea," he laughed.

"Good luck!" the female joked.

"Thanks," I said dully.

I turned around and called for everyone to follow me. They took off in my direction and I headed towards where they said Growan lived. There were almost no geese where the father goose had pointed and I was beginning to think he had lied to me, when Lexa asked me what was wrong with a goose on the ground near us.

"That's him," I said as I landed next to the goose. He was very unpreened and dirty and he was missing so many wing feathers that he looked like he couldn't fly. We landed near him. "Hello, are you Growan?" I asked, approaching him.

"Father, are you sure this is the right goose?" Sorra asked me.

"He looks as crazy as us. He's the one," I answered.

"Um, excuse me?" I asked. He quickly swung his head in our direction. Something seemed wrong with him, as if he had hit his head on a rock and never recovered.

"I'm Growan. Who're you? What kind of gooses are you?" he asked. His lack of proper language disgusted me.

"We are emperor geese. Can you help us?" I asked. "We need to get all of the geese in the flock to fly up." The sun began to set and I worried that we wouldn't have time.

He looked into the distance and seemed to be wondering about something.

"Can you help us?" I repeated. I was beginning to doubt my plan.

His head swung around. "With what?" He asked. I reluctantly and clearly repeated our idea.

"'Course. Follow me," he answered with a strange look in his eye as he started to waddle away weirdly. I didn't like this bird.

"If you want to scare the geese, I have a great idea for that. We just need to get a human to run into the flock. I used to do it when I was a chick. They always hated me for it," He laughed. "Follow me."

This time he started towards a human who was standing near its giant moving creature with four legs and that smelled like oil.

I stopped with everyone as Growan walked up to the human. The human didn't see him. "What are you doing?" I asked in a scream-whisper.

"Getting its attention."

"You're crazy!" Leyos yelled in his young male voice.

"Watch and learn, young'n," he honked back. Growan honked so that the human looked at him and turned around. Suddenly, Growan lurched at him and bit the strange feathers on its leg that the humans were always covered in. He pulled at them and almost tripped up the human. It made many loud noises and jumped around a lot.

I heard a fabric-like ripping sound and I saw the human grab its booming stick and point it at Growan. "Growan!" I yelled.

"Calm down, emperor! I'm a pro!" he honked after letting go of the human.

Just before the stick boomed and the deathberries flew out, Growan jumped to the side and shook his tail feathers at the human. It growled and pointed the stick at Growan again. He jumped to the side again and barely missed the deathberries. Suddenly, Growan took off into the flock, the human on his tail, still shooting deathberries. We jumped out of the way as they ran past us.

Just as Sorra had proposed, the geese flew into the sky like fall leaves being blown away by the wind. The thousands of geese took off as Growan and the human ran through them.

"Look for them!" Edel yelled. We all scanned the sky as the many geese took off. I only saw brown bellies and Canadians until I thought I saw a flash of grey.

"Hey, I think I see them!" I honked.

"There!" Sorra pointed with her beak as we saw six Emperor geese in the flocks of Canadians. I took off with Edel, Eiloo, and Lexa following me. We flew through the panicked geese and finally saw our chicks.

"Hey, Oulah! Plowu! Falu!" Lexa yelled.

"Get down here!" Eiloo honked. They saw us and gasped.

"Land!" I yelled angrily. Lexa looked at me and I remembered our conversation. I debated with myself if I would forget it or not.

The chicks dutifully landed on the ground with the other calming Canada geese. "H-how did you find us?" Plowu asked cautiously.

"Mounu! We aren't stupid, you know." Sorra yelled when she landed next to us. "Did you think you could leave us behind and get away with it?"

"Quiet, Sorra," I said.

"How dare you leave without telling us! You could have been killed!" Edel yelled.

"I'm just so glad you're okay," Lexa said as she hugged them.

"Dila, you are the responsible one. Why did you leave?" Eiloo asked.

"It was Tuah's chick's idea. They dragged me into it. They bet that we couldn't make it to Canada and we said that we could. Eventually we found Mounu and he told us how to get here," she answered.

"We just wanted to see the world like Father would have!" Falu whined.

"Well, you're not seeing any more of it! We are going home now," I honked. I looked for Growan but only saw an exhausted human returning to its creature with no dead goose and no booming stick. Growan must have escaped alive and I thanked him in my head.

"But the sun is setting, Father," Oulah said.

"Then we're flying at night! Come on!" I yelled as I jumped into the sky. Everyone took off behind me and we headed straight to the breeding grounds. The sun quickly set and the moon that was still half full was enough light to bring us home late the next day. We were mostly quiet on the way home and I was preparing their punishment and what I would and would not say to them.

- CHAPTER 26 -

"GOODBYE, TUAH AND THANKS for helping," Eiloo honked as he and his family broke off in the direction of their nest.

"Goodbye, Eiloo," I said. Soon, I landed next to our nest with Lexa and the chicks behind me. The trip was short and silent. Nobody needed to say anything. Morning had come and the breeding grounds were full of geese.

"Can you please give us some time alone?" I asked Sorra and Leyos. They nodded and flew onto the water in the marsh.

"We didn't mean to disobey you, Father, we just thought that you wouldn't be so mad at us because you almost left," Plowu bravely pleaded.

"Well, I am!" I honked.

"We're sorry, Fath --"

"You should be! You could have died! Did you not see all the humans there?" I yelled. I looked away at all the other geese that had recently arrived at the breeding grounds. "You three will stay at the nest until summer," I said.

"Tuah!" Lexa honked. "They are just young and adventurous, and, yes you should punish them but you can't blame them too much. They are kids. They still need their freedom."

I took a deep breath. Apparently, we would have to continue

our conversation in front of our chicks. "They should never have left at all! They caused us so much worry and we had to search for Mounu, fly overnight to Yukon, deal with humans to find them, and then we had to fly all the way back here. Are you saying I shouldn't be angry at them?" I asked.

"No, but I am saying not to punish them harshly!"

"They deserve to be punished!" I honked. Our chicks looked down. A tear may have even dropped from Oulah's eyes. I looked away and sighed.

"Father, don't we deserve freedom too?" Falu asked.

"Of course you deserve freedom, everyone does. But not that kind of freedom. You don't have the right to leave without asking permission!" Falu sighed.

Lexa still stood there in front of me, angrily. "Let me punish them."

"Fine!"

Lexa turned to face them. "You will be grounded until the middle of spring. And when I say grounded, I mean you can't fly unless there is an emergency. And if you are seen flying, your father will decide your next punishment. Got it?" she asked. They quietly nodded.

"I'm going to the water," Oulah said as her voice cracked. Plowu and Falu followed her. That was a quick conversation.

I was ashamed of them and regretful that I had yelled at Lexa. I flew to the water too, but not to the area where our chicks were. Lexa must have followed me, because she landed on the water behind me shortly after I landed. I took a sip of much needed water as my feet paddled me away from the shore.

"I'm sorry, Tuah. I love you, but I love them just as much. I can't let you punish them too much for being adventurous. I gave them about an extra month." Lexa said.

"I know."

"We have to cherish what we have," she whispered when she leaned her head against me.

The sun was setting and the marsh glowed with a picturesque beauty. The water turned orange and the grasses got a yellow tint on the sun facing side. A small flock of geese flew over and I suddenly felt the warm feeling of being home. I was in the place I belonged and there was nothing that got in the way.

I turned around and faced Lexa. "I'm sorry too. I just got so angry at them because I want to protect them. I shouldn't have yelled at you and I should have let you decide their punishment in the first place."

"It's okay, Tuah," she answered. I kissed her as the sun faded away and the stars looked upon the Earth. Everything was flawless for that one perfect moment. And I wanted it to stay that way forever, but Lexa pulled back slowly and opened her eyes and started back towards the nest.

I was left sitting alone on the water, wondering if there was an invisible wall between us because of me. She shook her tail off as she stepped out of the water and walked back up the hill to the nest. I looked at my reflection in the water. I knew I wasn't much to look at, but I still had my handsome breeding season feathers and I remembered what I was as the moment fully lost its grasp and faded away.

I looked up at the stars while I still sat on the water. Their reflections shimmered in the water. The sun had almost left and there was only a small light spot in the sky that didn't even reflect on the water that still held on. "Thank you for bringing them home safe, Parus," I whispered to the sky. Parus's star seemed to twinkle and I knew that she had heard me.

Lexa would worry if I didn't return home soon, so I swam over to the bank, shook the droplets of water off my tail feathers, and walked up to the nest. Lexa was already asleep with her wings spread over as many of her chicks as she could reach. I laid down on the other side of the nest and spread my wings over the chicks that Lexa hadn't covered.

Oulah was next to me and she peeked open her eyes as I sat down. "I really am sorry, Father," she whispered weakly.

"I know. It's okay, Oulah. Go back to sleep."

Her eyes closed and before I closed my eyes she was already back to sleep. I took one last look at the stars before I drifted away and said goodnight to my older sister, my younger sister, and my son. Fatigue took over and my eyelids grew heavy as I rested my head on my soft wing feathers and fell asleep.

- CHAPTER 27 -

WHEN I WOKE UP, the chicks had already gone looking for breakfast. Lexa was rearranging the nest as I stood up. "Good morning, Lexa."

"Good morning, Tuah," she said as she looked in my direction.

"Where are the chicks?"

"Oh, who knows. Probably visiting Eiloo's chicks and finding out what their punishment was or going to see the first chick that hatched this year. Speaking of chicks, were we going to have chicks this year or just continue to take care of our first brood?"

"Whatever you want. The first brood was so much to handle I don't know if we could take on more chicks," I answered.

"They would help us and we wouldn't have that much to do. And our first brood isn't that bad!" she laughed.

"I'm going to go eat," I said.

"Okay."

I walked down to the water to eat some of the soft, young grasses near the water. I lowered my head and came upon a berry in the water. It was floating by all itself and it seemed like it was waiting to know its destiny. And I knew the perfect bird who fulfil its destiny. I brought it back to Lexa as a gift and then went to visit Eiloo.

He told me that he firmly told his chicks that they were wrong to leave and that they should never do it again. Neither Eiloo nor Edel wanted to punish them any further than that. Edel had already fixed up the nest and laid her second clutch. She let me peek underneath her and I saw six perfect little eggs. I congratulated them and left to find my chicks. It took me a while to find them. I flew over the marsh and checked back at the nest and I started to wonder if they had left again, then I saw them at the berry bush where I first met Lexa.

I flew down and landed next to them. They were calmly eating berries and leaves next to the water. "Are you okay?" I asked them.

"Leyos and I are. Ask them," Sorra said, looking at Plowu, Falu, and Oulah.

"Look, we are really sorry, Father so can you just leave us alone for a while?" Falu asked. His tone wasn't angry but his words were hurtful.

"Okay. Don't you want to talk about it?" I asked. Falu shook his head. So much for trying to be a forgiving father.

"No," said Plowu.

"I'm sorry, Father. I think that is all we need to say," Oulah said. I did not expect that answer from her or any of them. I flew back to Lexa for guidance.

I found her drifting on the brackish marsh water alone. I waddled over to her and swam into the water. "Do you think I was too hard on them?" I asked when I got to her.

"They don't want to talk to me."

"Give them some time alone," she answered.

"At first, I thought fatherhood would be extremely difficult, but it seemed easier than I had expected as time went on. But, now that I think of it, it wasn't easier. It was just different. Everything has been so unexpected." I said.

"Yeah, a lot of it I didn't expect either. I was ready for it all, though. I was much more prepared than you were."

I chuckled. "You were always ready. Everything passed so fast for me. First, I wasn't ready, then I was suddenly a father. I guess I had to be ready."

"You're a good father, Tuah. I hope you know that."

"Thank you, Lexa." She smiled at me.

I looked around the breeding grounds. Most geese were either building or rebuilding nests or sitting on eggs. It was midday and clouds were nearing the sun. It was a quiet and calm environment, but I assumed that we would have a chaotic spring thunderstorm this evening.

This precise time of year felt significant. After a few minutes of thought, I guessed that today I had become four years old. "Hey, I think today's my birthday," I whispered. "My brood hatched early, when everyone else still had eggs."

"Wow. Happy birthday, Tuah!"

"Thanks."

As I had predicted, there was a thunderstorm that evening. We all huddled together at the nest and tried to stay as dry as possible. The wind wasn't so bad, but the rain poured all night and I never got to see the stars. I spread my wing over Lexa but the water still soaked through my feathers. No one got a good night of sleep.

A couple of weeks later, Lexa sat down on the nest and didn't get up. I brought her berries and fresh food and guarded the nest when she had to go drink water from the marsh. Lexa had laid five eggs. She incubated them for weeks and I was on high alert for danger. But little did I know, the spring peace would soon end.

I perked up when I heard the alarm call downhill. I had been preening near the nest and was not on alert. As soon as I heard Lexa, I leaped into the air and flew back to the nest at breakneck speed, but it was too late. The fox had already left with one precious egg. But Lexa and I moved on, as seasoned parents would.

Sometimes I would help turn our eggs over when I wasn't guarding and our chicks would bring Lexa food sometimes. They were very excited about the new chicks. They were very demanding though, and Lexa put all her time and energy into them. Sorra and Oulah helped a lot, and Lexa wouldn't have been able to take care of the eggs and our older chicks without them.

The older chicks had gotten over their punishment and were doing what they usually did this time of year. I had forgiven them, but I would never forget it. Lexa helped me to accept that they were children and they didn't make the best decisions all the time. And their punishment wasn't very bad. The middle of spring was almost here and they would be allowed to fly again.

The eggs were very close to hatching, and I occasionally noticed small cheeps from the eggs when Lexa would talk and sing to them. There were babies in there and the excitement of being a father returned again. There were already some chicks in the flock that were running around and having their first swim in the marsh. That evening, we were getting comfortable and preening around the nest while the sun set.

No one heard it coming that night, they are masters of nocturnal silence. Not one goose called the alarm call until it was right over us. It landed quietly on the ground and hooted loudly behind us. We jerked around and called the alarm call. It wasn't in the mood to fight. It had come to take what it wanted and no one was going to stop it. "Snowy owl!" I screamed.

The chicks immediately took off into the sky, calling the alarm call. Other geese around us took to the sky in panic as well. Lexa stood up on the nest, hissing and I saw that two chicks had just finished hatching. The owl hooted and started walking towards her.

"Lexa, fly! You know you can't fight it!" I yelled. I flew to her and pushed her off the nest and away from the owl.

"The chicks!" she honked. I couldn't let her be eaten by an owl. She flapped her wings as hard as she could and fought me with all her strength, but my will was stronger. I held her down while the owl approached the nest.

"No, Tuah!" she yelled.

"Fly! Go!" I said, pushing her into the sky. The owl had already taken the two chicks and destroyed the rest of the eggs. The owl glanced back at us with bright, fierce, orange eyes and I looked deep into them. He was a father just like me, but he didn't think twice about me. He was not a human. He would not let his species die because he was guilty about raiding some noble goose's nest. He took off and his mighty wings caused the air around him to swirl and form invisible tornadoes.

"No!" Leyos screamed from the sky. I sighed and looked down. I closed my eyes. After a few deep breaths, I walked back to the nest to find Lexa leaning over the destroyed nest. Eggshells littered the ground and yolk was dotted in a few spots.

"It could have killed us and our first clutch, Lexa," I said. She looked at the eggs. One was a dud and only had yolk in it, but the other two had little unhatched chicks in them.

"Oh," she said shakily.

I looked up to make sure the snowy owl was gone. There was no sign of it. The sun was about to finish setting. Our chicks flew back to the ground and saw the nest. "The eggs!" Plowu honked. Oulah looked at them and started to cry. Falu looked away and Leyos looked down. Sorra landed last and cried with Oulah. Lexa was still in shock standing next to the nest and I wanted to preserve my shock until everyone else was okay.

"Oh, Father!" Sorra cried. "They were so close!"

The last of the sun's light vanished. "Come on, let's get ready to sleep," I said.

"How can we sleep now?" Falu asked.

"By closing your eyes and resting." They walked to their spots where they slept and laid down.

"Come on, Lexa," I said, moving her away from the nest. She was talking quietly to herself while I sat her down and told her to sleep. She quickly fell asleep with the rest of the chicks.

After I had put the family to sleep, I flew to the water and floated there, alone. The stars were out tonight and they watched over us. My shock finally came and faded away and I started to cry. I watched my reflection in the water while the tears poured into the marsh. As much as I loved having family in the sky watching over me, I missed them and now I would have more children in the stars. I looked up and the tears streamed down the side of my face instead of dripping off my beak. I searched for the stars that would be my five chicks of that brood and said goodnight to them. I quieted my crying and listened to the sounds of the marsh. It was very dark and the moon was only a sliver of light, but I could still see everything I needed to see. I took a deep breath and washed my face off in the marsh, then returned to the destroyed nest and fell asleep with my family.

- CHAPTER 28 -

I WOKE UP TO the sound of them talking, but I kept my eyes closed and listened. I heard my brother's voice with them. "He was very brave to do what none of us had the strength to do." Lexa said.

Who? I wondered.

"If he would have let me go, I probably would have become prey to the owl along with the chicks. I just, couldn't let them go," she said. I knew who she was talking about.

"Tuah is like that. I'm just so relieved that none of you got hurt," said Eiloo.

"We're all very sad about the chicks," Plowu whispered.

"You could lay another clutch," Leyos said.

"No, it's too late in the season. They might not be able to migrate in time," she answered.

"I'm very sorry. But I need to get back to Edel to make sure that this doesn't happen to our eggs," Eiloo honked.

"Yes. Thank you, Eiloo," Lexa said. I heard him fly away.

I opened my eyes and stood up. "Oh, good morning, Tuah," Lexa said drearily.

"Is everyone okay?" I asked. They all nodded except for Oulah.

"Not the babies," Oulah said, looking at the nest.

I sighed. "Did you clean the nest up?"

"Yes, the egg shells are gone," Plowu answered.

"Are you okay, Tuah?" Lexa asked. I nodded.

"You three can fly now. Your punishment is over," I said, looking at Oulah, Falu, and Plowu. They smiled a little.

"I'm going to the water," Falu said. He took off and took his time making it to the water.

"What do we do now that the eggs are gone?" Sorra asked.

"Nothing," I answered. "Eiloo has plenty of help so we don't need to help him, so we just wait until next spring. You don't have to stay with us all the time because we don't have the eggs anymore."

"We will stay, Father," Leyos answered.

"I feel useless, Tuah," Lexa said. The chicks had left and we were still at the nest.

"At least try to find something to do instead of sitting around, looking at the nest."

"What is there to do? I've eaten, swam, and caught up on sleep. I don't know what else to do."

I had an idea. "I'll be right back," I said.

I flew down to the water and plucked a berry from the berry bush and brought it back to Lexa. I dropped the berry at her feet. She sighed. "Thank you, Tuah," she said sadly after eating the berry.

I hugged her. "We'll be fine. We can find something to do with our spare time," I said.

"It's not just that, Tuah. I miss them," she whispered.

"Do you want to spend more time with our first brood?"

"Maybe that will help," she shook her head. "I just need to get over it."

"Okay."

Spring passed quickly. The chicks loved being older in the breeding grounds. They would try to count how many chicks were in the entire flock or befriend as many as possible. They still watched out for Lexa and made sure that she was okay. What made her happier in the end was the thought that she would get to lay another clutch next year.

Summer burned through and greened the grass. It was another good year, except for the humans that intruded closer and closer into our breeding grounds. We all gathered in sorrow when the first goose was killed by the human's deathberries. He was a father, and his mate had to raise their seven chicks by herself and their chicks would never have a father to guard them. My stomach twisted and turned at the sight of the mangled body covered in blood.

The only thing that wasn't completely horrible about losing the chicks was that I didn't have to bring the dead ones to the edge of the colony. I didn't have to see the foxes and minks and eagles that waited for their food. Soon, Autumn began to blow cold winds from the arctic over Alaska. The bone-chilling breezes and darkening skies alerted us that it was almost time to go. We filled our bellies to the maximum every day to prepare for the flight. I watched as the new chicks from this year learned how to fly and prepared to migrate with us. They were so wonderful in the way that they followed their parent's every action and the joy they experienced when they first got into the sky was indescribable.

I thought about how I would have been one of those parents teaching their chicks to fly if that owl hadn't attacked our nest. It had come so quickly and left so quickly. All I could think about when I thought about that was that there was nothing else I could have done.

I watched one night from our nest as the young chicks gathered together to see the elder and learn the dangers of humans. This time, she seemed angry that the humans were affecting our way of life and I remembered what the Canada goose colony looked like. If she would have seen that colony, she would have died, considering the way she spoke of our problem.

I didn't hear most of her words. I said goodnight to the stars and tucked my head underneath my wing feathers. Lexa was already beside me, falling asleep and the chicks were around us in their favorite spots to rest. They would fight over the softer bedding areas and compete to see who would get to sleep there. It was amusing to watch them argue, but I would have to step in if things got too rough.

Eiloo's first and second clutches were very ready for migration to the wintering grounds and I watched them fly over our nest occasionally. The nights became colder and soon we gathered together to migrate.

"Are you ready?" Lexa asked everyone.

"This isn't our first time migrating, Mother! Of course, we're ready," Falu answered.

A group of geese took off to our right. When the geese in our group took off, we spread our wings and lifted off the grassy Alaskan marshlands. I heard honking around us as we got into our v's and our flight patterns Southward. I led our v first, then everyone else rotated around. I saw the land I had seen every time I had migrated move underneath me. I yearned to be young again and see the world for the first time, but I wanted nothing more than to have my chicks migrating with me.

- CHAPTER 29 -

WE FLEW ALL DAY and rested in the evening. We were right next to the ocean and when I woke up, I thought we were already in the wintering grounds. One look around told me that we hadn't made it yet. We quickly got up and continued the journey. Our silence was broken by the sounds of a goose colony. The geese honked and flapped around as they taught the young ones what foods to eat here and scrambled to get themselves food. We found a spot close to my rock and arranged the sleeping areas. Lexa seemed to have fully recovered from losing our eggs and was back to her normal self, but I flew to my rock and obtained some much-needed peace of mind.

The ocean slammed up against the rocks and misted me while the sun failed to warm the salt water off my body in the cool Autumn air. I listened to the northern gulls while they flapped around. A cloud passed over the sun and the wintering grounds darkened while more mist cooled me ever more. I shivered slightly from the cool wind and gathered near the rest of the geese to stay warmer. Then, I saw a flock of snow geese fly in and I thought I recognized one. I waddled over to where they had landed and got a better look at the goose. He had sat down and was preening his feathers with everyone else.

"Bruna?" I asked. "Is that you?" He looked up at me.

"Hey! I remember you! What was your name?" Bruna asked.

"Tuah."

"Yes! I remember now! How are you? I haven't seen you in years!" he honked.

"I'm good. Is Dailin still following you around, scaring everyone off?"

He laughed. "No, she has her own family now and I am afraid she is going to raise her chicks to be as mean as her! So, tell me what's been going on."

We sat down together and talked about everything that had happened since the day we met. He never had a mate or chicks, he just lived alone. I asked him how he did that without falling in love with someone and he said that that's just the way he was and he enjoyed being by himself. I told him about when the chicks flew to Canada and he said he wished he could have been here to help.

"You should know that your story has traveled through our colonies and geese look up to you." He said.

"Really? What story?" I laughed.

"You're a hero, Tuah. No one has ever fought an eagle, made it to the wintering grounds injured, and done all the other noble things you have done."

"The eagle fight was a team effort. Actually, all of it was. I have always had family and friends to help me through it. I just got recognized because I carried everything out."

"No! You have become a story that parents tell their chicks!" I scoffed when he said that. I wasn't the least bit brave when I was on the brink of death. I just followed my instincts and let my reflexes take control.

That night, before I returned to Lexa, I showed him the stars I believed were my family in the sky. I expected him to think I was crazy, but he truly and heartfeltly believed it like Lexa and Eiloo. He pointed to stars that were his family who had died and even shed a tear or two remembering his father. He said his father had died defending their nest when they were nestlings and he would never forget him. I was happy to know that I had given him another way to remember him.

I told him the story of Jounu and how I was enraged at the scavengers that waited for food. They cheated nature by taking the freshly dead instead of attacking and trying to kill their own food or eating a vegetarian diet. Bruna said that if we didn't give them our dead chicks, then there would be more attacks and maybe even adults that died. I believed him, but I still would never like giving them my chicks. Bruna told me about how much the humans affected his life. They occasionally killed but mostly watched them from afar with strange machines.

I asked him what machines were and he told me that they are things that the humans use for something. I didn't pay much attention to the part about groups of people trying to spot the Snow geese and then how they documented them with more machines. I said that they have too much to do with our lives and that they should leave us alone. Bruna was surprised about the Canadian goose colony having the number of humans it had, but not for the reason I thought. He said that his grandfather had seen thousands upon thousands of Canadians killed. I didn't like humans at all.

Soon, Lexa came to find me and I introduced her to Bruna. It was already very late and I returned to our chicks with Lexa while Bruna gathered with the other Snow geese. It was turning out to be a great winter after all.

The next day, I took a required bath in the ocean. Lexa said that I stank. (I told her that it was the grouping of all the geese and poop that she smelled, but she insisted it was me.) I struggled against the waves to clean all my feathers off while I ducked underwater. I walked out of the ocean and shook my feathers violently while I tried to get the salt off too. It didn't work. I was thankful that my feathers are waterproof and it was only my feathers that were sticky and salty and not my skin.

It would be the chicks' first breeding year when they returned to the breeding grounds and they were all ready for their spring feathers. They seemed to be around Lexa and I less but that just gave us more time to plan how we would better be on owl lookout next year. Every ten minutes, Lexa would look around and check for an owl. And I would have to always be on danger alert and be on owl lookout every five minutes. It sounded very exhausting when you included the owl lookout. Everything was going fine, until I had another one of my nightmares that night.

I dreamed that weights were tying me down in a dark, grey land. Everything was foggy and I heard humans calling. Lexa screamed for help from somewhere, and I couldn't find where she was. I felt alone and helpless and the lack of my ability to fly made me feel like I was in a tiny cage and most of my world was on the other side of the bars. I called for her, and she didn't respond. I tried to fly up to look for her, but my wings were still

glued to the ground. I couldn't lift them into the air and the atmosphere felt still and depressing, yet it seemed to be spinning. I
felt trapped and scared and I remembered that I had felt this way
during my first winter. The snow had been swirling around me
and confused me and Lexa had been calling for me somewhere
in the sky. My chest pounded and my ability to move at all was
decreasing. I thought I was going to die, when I heard Lexa say
something else.

"Wake up, Tuah!" she honked.

I jumped up and tore my eyes open as the sunlight forced
them closed again. "What? What happened? Is everyone all
right?" I asked, stumbling around a little.

"We are fine, Father," Sorra said calmly.

The tone in her voice helped me calm down and I sat back
down and slowly opened my eyes in the sunlight. "Are you okay,
Tuah?" Lexa asked.

"Yeah, I'm fine. Just a nightmare," I answered. I assumed I
must have slept into the morning.

"About what?" Leyos asked.

"It was nothing, I'm okay."

"We're almost adults now, Father. You don't have to hide stuff
from us anymore." Oulah said. I sighed.

"I know, Oulah. But this I just want to keep between Lexa and
me."

"Come on, let's go get something to eat," Plowu asked, seeing
that I didn't want to tell them about my dream. I thanked her in
my head while they flew away and turned to Lexa.

"What was it? You were freaking out," she said.

"It was another one of those dreams about not being able to fly. It was foggy and you were calling for help and humans were coming I think, but I couldn't save you because my wings were too heavy," I answered.

"It was just a dream, Tuah."

"This one seemed so real I almost felt like it was a memory," I said. Tears pooled in my eyes.

"Dreams rarely become reality-,"

"I hope this one doesn't," I said quickly as my voice cracked.

"Tuah," Her tone was pleading and sad. "I thought you weren't afraid anymore. I was proud of you." I suddenly felt ashamed of myself, but I couldn't help what I dreamed or that I would always seek help from her.

"I'm not afraid, it just startled me. I'm sorry I told you."

"No, you can tell me anything. I just thought you had out-grown that." She said.

"Me too."

I visited with Bruna again the next day and finished our long conversation. I didn't tell him about my dream, I decided to keep it just between Lexa and me. The chicks didn't ask about my dream again and continued to drift farther away from us.

It was midwinter now, and snow fell lightly on the rocky beaches. I sat with Lexa on my favorite rock. "Do you think they are spending less time with us because of me?" I asked.

"No! They're growing up. And they are almost adults."

"I can't believe that."

"Me neither." She said.

- CHAPTER 30 -

"HOW ARE YOU, BROTHER?" I asked Eiloo. I had gone to visit him and his family.

"We're great. The chicks are wonderful and just being themselves and Edel is enjoying her last season with our chicks."

"Good," I said.

"How are *you*?" he asked.

I sighed. "I've been better. I had another nightmare like the ones I used to have, but this time there was only one. Usually I have them in a row," I answered.

"Why do you keep having them?"

I shook my head. "I wish I knew. Maybe it is the fear of not being able to fly and protect my family that is always in the back of my mind. That might be causing the dreams."

"I think that if you think of the past you are more likely to have dreams about it. Have you talked about the past or thought about it?" he asked.

"I talked to an old friend about it."

"That's probably why. You have remembered the dreams like you remembered being left in the breeding grounds," he honked.

"I wasn't left, Lexa was with me. And this dream seemed so real, like it wasn't because of remembering the past, I feel like it was something else…"

I fought for peace in my mind on my rock by myself one night. I looked up at the stars and begged for relief. I couldn't get the thought out of my head. I knew this was different and I felt like something was coming, but I didn't know what. "Please sister, don't let it become real," I pleaded. Parus's star only twinkled like the rest and refused to reveal any sign of answer. I looked to all of them desperately, but I only found loneliness in looking at them.

"I can't wait for something terrible to happen, I know that this dream was different. You are the only geese I can talk to who understand, and you are millions of miles away!" I yelled. "Why did you have to die?" I cried. Between my sobbing, I whispered, "Please, tell me." I looked up and the stars only danced across my eyes as the tears stretched their shimmering. I looked down at the rock I was sitting on and felt none of the peace I was in urgent need of.

As more time passed, more nightmares tormented my mind. Geese gave me all the assistance they could give- I was going through my midlife crisis, I just remembered the past, it would pass soon. I didn't know why this was happening or what was going on. I thought my struggles in life had ended, but I could feel more were coming.

The weather warmed, and I only felt worse. Lexa tried to help, but her assistance only aggravated my condition. I couldn't imagine life without her, but in my dreams, I couldn't save her. Eiloo's voice was muted in my ears and only Sorra of all geese, seemed to help ease the pain. I don't know why, but her voice seemed to make everything better when she tried to help me.

I was ashamed to have to be this way in front of my chicks, but Sorra didn't seem to mind. I couldn't hide the fact that I was guilty of seeming to favor her, but there was nothing I could do. I asked the stars every night for guidance but their shining and twinkling almost drove me insane. The only feelings I felt were the feelings of momentary relief from Sorra and the destructing feeling of failure within me. I must have done something wrong. I knew something was coming, I was about to lose something, but I never knew what, until it was time to migrate again.

The flocks took off one by one into the sky and soon, our family v was in the sky heading Northward. We gained two more birds in our family, Dulon and Naula. Falu was always with Naula and Plowu never left Dulon's side. Our chicks had grown their breeding season feathers along with Lexa and me. I didn't notice my feathers until I arrived in the breeding grounds after the long migration.

The more we flew, the more on edge I became. Whispers of death echoed in my head. I looked up to the sky to try to tell myself that even during the day the stars were up there, but fog had covered my view of the sky and we were about to fly into a large cloud of fog. I looked at it in fear and I knew that we shouldn't fly in there, but I couldn't find the words to speak. Nonetheless, we entered the foggy mass. Everything was peaceful inside and the chicks seemed to enjoy it. I didn't. I felt like I could smell death in it, and it clogged my throat and I couldn't speak. I felt like I was failing in being a father again, but I only kept flying.

I continued to panic, trying to calm myself down. I took a few deep breaths and looked around. We were surrounded by thick fog, but I could tell which direction were going. I noticed that it was just our family and Naula and Dulon with us. Suddenly, I thought I heard a sound below us and I quickly flew a little higher as I looked down. Everyone seemed fine and I didn't see anything below us.

Finally, I couldn't take it anymore and breathed a word, "Lexa," I whispered. Anxiety kept it quiet.

She looked back at me. "Yes, Tuah?" she asked.

"We need to get out…"

Boom!

The sounds of the human sticks that spit deathberries rang in my ears. I saw them fly through the sky like lightning and slice the fog. The air exploded with booms and panic. I sped up my flying to try to escape the fog, but it seemed to go on forever. Deathberry after deathberry shot through the sky.

The chicks screamed and I heard someone honk, and a goose fell from the sky. I didn't know who it was and I was about to dive down to save them when I found Lexa next to me. Another ear-piercing boom rang out and I looked to Lexa after I winced. Then, she wasn't next to me and I looked down as she disappeared into the fog. "Lexa!" I screamed as I looked down. I dove to the ground as fast as I could.

Oulah flew down behind me. The ground was suddenly just below me and I pulled up. I landed and saw the shadows of humans nearing, and my heart raced. I found Lexa laying on the ground and I ran to her. "Lexa, Lexa!" I yelled to her.

Her head was laying at a lopsided angle and her wings were spread out. My eyes caught her chest and I saw blood covering a wound. "A deathberry!" I said in horror. Oulah screamed and began to cry behind me when she saw it. She was standing a few yards behind me.

"Tuah," she struggled to say.

"Don't talk, Lexa. We are going to get you out of here."

"They're coming, Father!" Oulah yelled.

I heard another boom and turned to look at Oulah. I gasped when I saw her laying limp on the ground with fresh blood on her chest where the deathberry had hit her. I looked back to Lexa when she spoke.

"Tuah, leave me," Lexa breathed. Her body seemed weak and small. Feathers floated in the air around us like little angels coming to take her away. Blood was everywhere and it scared me more than anything else.

"No, you stayed with me when I was injured. I am going to stay with you now," I answered.

"Tuah, listen,"

"No, you listen!"

"Stop, Tuah," she coughed.

"No, I have to get you out of here!" I yelled.

"Tuah, listen!" she wheezed. "Do you love me?" she asked. The words almost brought tears to my eyes and it almost ripped my heart out to remember her saying that the first time.

"Of course I do, Lexa."

"Then leave and take care of the ones you love for me," she breathed.

I heard the humans walk closer. The blood on Lexa's chest started to drip down her side. I looked in the direction the humans were and back at Lexa. Her eyes started to turn grey and their beautiful light started to fade as she looked at me. "I love you, Lexa," I said as I gently kissed her forehead and started to run to take off.

I looked back at her and my heart that lived within my freedom-filled wings felt like they were being tied down by ropes and I couldn't take off. But my heart wanted to fulfil what Lexa had told me to do for her couldn't let me stay. I was torn apart trying to leave her and love her at the same time. I saw Oulah and I knew that I had failed in doing my job. Thoughts started to race through my head as I flew through the cloud of fog. That was the only reason I was blessed with Lexa and chicks, because I was entrusted to take care of them, and I didn't.

My life seemed useless and the only reason I ever lived was to keep my rare species as far away from extinction, and I hadn't even succeeded in that. Lexa's body showed no sign of life as I looked back at her and Oulah had died instantly. They were gone, and now I had more family living in the dreadful night sky. I was alone. My mate was gone, and I had failed.

I heard another boom and I felt a sharp pain in my right flank, just above my leg. I screamed as the pain spread through my entire leg and I lifted the weights on my wings as high as I could and flapped them harder and harder until I had gained enough altitude to glide. I didn't glide though; I flew faster and faster while the pain in my flank still burned more than the sun.

"No, no, no, no!" I cried as I remembered my dream. I fell to the ground and crashed on my side. "No!" I yelled as I looked back towards the fog that was now miles away. Tears streamed down my eyes. "No!"

All I could say was no, and all I could think about was how similar the dream and now the memory felt. I cried as hard as I could when I remembered Lexa saying that dreams rarely become reality and the one time she was wrong, she was gone when it came. The pain within me was more excruciating than the pain in my flank. I could feel that I would survive that wound, but I would never heal from the wound of losing Lexa.

I screamed as I looked back in the direction of my life that was now gone. I had no idea if anyone else had survived besides me. I wished I hadn't survived. I wished that the deathberry that penetrated my flank had pierced my heart and I would feel the amount of pain physically that I felt emotionally now, or I wouldn't have felt any at all. "Lexa," I wheezed. "No..."

- CHAPTER 31-

I GASPED AWAKE THE next day. The sun was already mid-sky and it made the rocky grasslands and distant mountains look like a desolate desert. I groaned as I felt the pain in my flank return. I looked down and saw dried blood on the ground and on my leg. I quickly remembered everything that had happened. The fog in the distance was gone and I quickly stood up to take off but got lightheaded and fell down. I rested my head on the ground until I was ready to stand up again. This time I got up slower and didn't fall down.

I took off in the direction of where the attack was yesterday. With the fog gone, I was able to better find where Lexa and Oulah were killed. I landed in the same area and shivered with the thought that I was standing in this exact same spot where Oulah was when she died. I looked down and only saw a little bit of dried blood on the dead grasses in the areas where they were killed. They were gone. I assumed that the humans had taken their bodies, because scavengers wouldn't be able to drag off two fully grown geese.

Tears filled my eyes, but my whimpering stopped when I noticed another small area of blood. I ran to it and noticed two more right next to it. "No, no, no," I said, wondering who else had been killed. I sat down to process all that had happened. "I have to get back to the breeding grounds," I said to myself. The survivors would have gone there and I could find them. I took off, heading North once again.

I hoped with all my heart that the blood spots were geese that were injured and somehow made it to the breeding grounds. I swallowed the pain from my flank. It wasn't going to stop me from getting to the breeding grounds. I didn't notice the land as I flew over it. I was too deep in my thoughts. I just let my instinct take me to where I needed to be, but I still had to pay attention to wind currents and my altitude.

It seemed to take forever, but I finally arrived in the marshy wetlands that were my home. I flew to our nest as fast as I could and found only Plowu, Sorra, and Naula waiting there for me. "Father!" Sorra said as she ran to me and hugged me. "I'm so glad you are okay. Where is Mother?" she asked. Tears filled my eyes and Sorra instantly understood. We just stood there for a minute and looked at each other sadly.

"Mother didn't make it?" Plowu said stepping forward.

I shook my head. Plowu looked down. "I'm sorry," Naula said. Her voice showed that she had been crying too.

"What about Oulah? And Falu and Leyos?" Sorra asked pleadingly.

"Oulah died yesterday when she tried to help me save Lexa. I saw three other spots of blood besides theirs. That must have been Falu, Leyos, and Dulon." Plowu started to cry and Sorra stood, staring at nothing and trying to figure out everything. I laid down next to the nest to rest.

"Father, your leg," Plowu said looking at me.

"I'm fine. It's nothing compared to what else I feel."

"Well, I'll leave you with just family. I need to go tell my parents what happened and recover too. I am so very sorry about what happened," Dulon said before he flew away.

"It's just us," Plowu said. It was past mid-day and the sun was lowering.

"We are never alone, Plowu. We can talk to them tonight in the stars and see them fly across the sky," I said.

Sorra nodded. "I want to do that."

"Me too," Plowu said through tears.

"What do we do now?" Sorra asked.

"We stick together, right Father?"

I nodded sadly. I laid in the same spot the rest of the day. I didn't eat, but I didn't sleep either. Sorra brought Eiloo to us and we told him all our different sides of the story. Edel came to help as well, and I remembered my dream again. "It was just like my dream, Eiloo," I said, still laying limply on the ground.

He gasped when he thought about it. "Wow, I guess you dreamed the future. I would be lying to say it must be a coincidence." he answered. "I'm so sorry, Tuah. They are in the stars now, though. Just like you said."

I saw three new stars in the sky near Selu's. I stared at Lexa's all night and wondered if I could will her back down to Earth. She stayed put in the sky. I wailed in sadness as I watched her star shimmer and gleam as more tears streamed down my face.

I felt so alone and failed. I wasn't ready to feel angry at the humans yet, I was too drowned in my sorrow-filled tears.

The days went by blandly. I seemed to recover slowly, but I was mostly quiet and slow moving. I didn't fly anywhere, I managed to force myself to the water to clean, and I only thought about everything I had lost. I watched the reeds shift in the wind and the world move as it always had, but I didn't find peace. I only felt longing, but I knew that what my dream had told me was not over. One more thing was coming.

Sorra and Plowu stayed very close to me and watched out for me all the time. They would bring me food when I didn't feel like walking to the good grasses, they reminded me to preen every once and a while, and they even fixed the nest up so that it looked more like home. One day, Plowu brought me some berries to eat, and I burst out in tears remembering Lexa. I explained to her why I was crying and she vowed never to bring me berries again. They only wanted to make me better, they didn't have room to make me worse.

One day, Sorra said to me, "I won't lay this year. I need to take care of you."

"Why? It might make things better to have more family."

"No, Father. I need to stay here with you," she answered.

"Thank you, Sorra."

Plowu was still so devastated that Dulon had died, she wasn't going to breed this year either. Neither of them asked me if I was. They knew the answer for this year, but they didn't know about any other year. I would never mate again. Lexa was the one and only, and now she was gone. Now I would fly alone like many other geese.

I felt older this year. My young heart was gone and my freedom-filled wings were limp by my side. I felt empty all the time.

There was a hole within me that was torn open when I saw the light fade from Lexa's eyes. Now, nothing but her could fill it and make me whole again. I had been torn apart and my other half was in the sky. I told Eiloo about this and he said that maybe if I flew, I would be closer to my other half, and that it would help me recover. I thought about it, but when I tried to fly, my wings became too heavy to lift and my sorrows didn't let me get more than a few feet off the ground. I hoped for something that would cause me to fly again. But I expected to never find it.

I walked around the colony instead of flying and it helped me get away from the nest. I looked away when I saw happy couples with their family as the memories rushed back. I rarely smiled. I was just quiet. For weeks.

One day, I saw a human near the other geese and I just looked at it. I didn't know what to think. It didn't see me, it just seemed to be minding its own business. It didn't look like it wanted to kill any of us. It was just there.

I talked to Lexa every night and told her about how Plowu and Sorra were doing. I told her how alive and wonderful the breeding grounds seemed, as they did every year. I always told her I missed her and wished we were together. Eiloo came by a lot to check on me, and Sorra never left my side unless I wanted to be alone.

The years passed slowly. Plowu met another goose that she loved even more than Dulon, but she still talked to him as an old friend in the sky. She had seven wonderful chicks who adored their aging grandfather. When my breeding season feathers returned every spring, they slowly became less handsome and some even fell off occasionally.

Sorra met a fine goose named Cambu. He wasn't an Emperor goose; he was a Brant. He was the first Brant I had ever met and he had a black head and the black feathers went all the way down to his chest. His eyes and beak were dark and his body was brown and white with a white tail and black wings. He had a necklace of white on his neck too, which made him even more striking. Sorra was reluctant to leave me at first, but when I was able to care for myself more, she drifted away and built her own family, and I was happy for her and proud of her. Cambu was the father of her two chicks that survived to adulthood. They were beautiful mixes with a mixture of white and black and brown. I always loved when they visited me.

Lexa was always with me. I was alone on Earth, but in time I came to learn that I was in good company in my heart. I lived in peace with the other emperor geese and my story spread farther than I could ever imagine. Multiple species carried it on into many different languages around the world. I rested with the other old geese and even became the elder who taught the juveniles about humans before they migrated for the first time. I was very proud of my position and family. Sorra and Plowu were happy, and although was never in life truly happy again without Lexa, I was as happy as I could be on Earth. I never met anyone else my age that I loved. I only loved Lexa and my chicks and their chicks. I saw Cambu and Plowu's mate as good friends. I was now eleven years old.

You could easily see it by looking at me. Not many geese reached the age I had become, and I held my position as elder goose long past the day when my expected successor died. I met my great-grandchicks and took very good care of them when their parents were resting. They loved to hear my stories, but I cautioned them when I told them about Canada. Mounu was long gone, and I told them of his story as well.

I became teary eyed when I told them about their great-grandmother. I taught them how the stars held our loved ones safe when they died and I told them of their aunts and uncles and long-perished family. I made sure they never forgot them. I told them how a brave goose named Parus had been protected by their great great-grandfather, but she then was killed by humans that same year. I never became angry at the humans for what they did to me and my family. The anger never passed through my scar that healed just fine. But I knew that the deathberry was still inside me, and until I died, it would still remind me of Lexa. It was my own symbol of the past, like a scar you look to and remember. When the chicks grew older, they suffered in their own ways from losing family to fighting to the death for their families. I helped them through all their struggles until I died.

Sorra lived with me until I reached my dying age. Parus died from old age before I did, which I mourned over. I could tell something was coming, like when I lost Lexa, but it was much more peaceful. A good thing was about to happen. She died happily and peacefully with her chicks and mate close to her.

I opened my eyes when another morning arrived. I looked up as I had when I first saw the world and saw the vast marshes and the sun rising over them as it did every day. I felt the cool Alaskan breeze brush past and dance with the grass. I heard the bustle of the goose colony and I felt the feeling I cherished my whole life. I was home and I had my family with me. There was nothing more that I ever truly wanted. Sorra returned from eating breakfast and we looked at each other during a moment of silence. It was time, and she knew it too. I laid down on the soft grasses of the breeding grounds, on the same dirt I hatched on many, many years ago. My legs had become weak and could hardly walk anymore, let alone allow me to fly.

Sorra, slightly worried, rushed over to me and listened to my words with love. I looked up at her. "Listen to me, Sorra, my only living daughter," I said.

"Yes, Father?" she asked, looking intently at me.

"Remember the ones who have passed, but do not feel sorrow for them, for they are in the stars now. I will see you one day when you perish and we will fly together as a family in the night sky. While you are still here, be good to the world, and take care of the ones you love for me." I held her wing. "Because when it is all over, the ones you love and that love you back are what matter most in life." I rested my head on the Earth I was hatched on and closed my eyes and was finally complete.

As he closed his eyes, I, his daughter, felt peace within me and I knew that he had joined my mother in the stars and every night I would look up and see them fly together happily, like two halves that had once again become a whole.

Author Note

Emperor geese like Tuah are a near-threatened species. This means that their population is decreasing quickly. Hunting, coastal oil pollution, and competition among brood rearing geese are all factors that are decreasing their population. If we don't save our rare species of the world, they will be gone forever and there will be no more geese to spread the story of the brave Tuah.

Emperor geese are managed cooperatively by the U.S Fish and Wildlife Service and the Alaska Department of Fish and Game. Please do your part to obey hunting rules and regulations. If you can, please donate to the Cornell Lab of Ornithology or get involved at birds.cornell.edu to protect disappearing birds like the Emperor goose and they will be around for us to marvel in their miraculous beauty for years to come.

About the Author

Jeyda Kathryn Bolukbasi is a fourteen-year-old writer who was born in Charlotte, NC. Her passion for birds sparked the inspiration for her first published book, Tuah, which she wrote when she was thirteen. She hopes to attend Cornell University and study to become an ornithologist. Currently, she is the first junior volunteer at the Center for Birds of Prey in Awendaw, SC and a member of the Carolina Bird Club.

Made in the USA
Columbia, SC
12 November 2019